"Clearly I can't maintain professional distance with you anymore."

"Shelby, you don't want to go and quit. I like you. I don't want to have to go breaking in someone new when we're getting along so well."

"We're getting along *too* well," she mumbled.

"I'll be good. No more touching. I'll even go back to calling you Ms. Dorset."

"I'm sorry, Gavin, but my mind's made up. I can't compromise my ethics. I'll make sure you get someone nice," she added.

"Well, if you're sure."

"I am."

"In that case…"

The next thing she knew, he was kissing her.

Dear Harlequin Intrigue Reader,

To mark a month of fall festivals, screeching goblins and hot apple cider, Harlequin Intrigue has a provocative October lineup guaranteed to spice things up!

Debra Webb launches her brand-new spin-off series, COLBY AGENCY: INTERNAL AFFAIRS, with *Situation: Out of Control*. This first installment sets the stage for the most crucial mission of all…smoking out a mole in their midst. The adrenaline keeps flowing in *Rules of Engagement* by acclaimed author Gayle Wilson, who continues her PHOENIX BROTHERHOOD series with a gripping murder mystery that hurls an unlikely couple into a vortex of danger.

Also this month, a strictly business arrangement turns into a lethal attraction, in *Cowboy Accomplice* by B.J. Daniels—book #2 in her Western series, McCALLS' MONTANA. And just in time for Halloween, October's haunting ECLIPSE selection, *The Legacy of Croft Castle* by Jean Barrett, promises to put you in that spooky frame of mind.

There are more thrills to come when Kara Lennox unveils the next story in her CODE OF THE COBRA series, with *Bounty Hunter Redemption,* which pits an alpha male lawman against a sexy parole officer when mayhem strikes. And, finally this month, watch for the action-packed political thriller *Shadow Soldier* by talented newcomer Dana Marton. This debut book spotlights an antiterrorist operative who embarks on a high-stakes mission to dismantle a diabolical ticking time bomb.

Enjoy!

Denise O'Sullivan
Senior Editor
Harlequin Intrigue

BOUNTY HUNTER REDEMPTION

KARA LENNOX

HARLEQUIN®

TORONTO • NEW YORK • LONDON
AMSTERDAM • PARIS • SYDNEY • HAMBURG
STOCKHOLM • ATHENS • TOKYO • MILAN • MADRID
PRAGUE • WARSAW • BUDAPEST • AUCKLAND

ISBN 0-373-22805-8

BOUNTY HUNTER REDEMPTION

Copyright © 2004 by Karen Leabo

ABOUT THE AUTHOR

Texas native Kara Lennox has been an art director, typesetter, textbook editor and reporter. She's worked in a boutique, a health club and an ad agency. She's been an antiques dealer and even a blackjack dealer. But no work has made her happier than writing romance novels.

When not writing, Kara indulges in an ever-changing array of weird hobbies. (Her latest passions are treasure hunting and creating mosaics.) She loves to hear from readers. You can visit her Web site and drop her a note at www.karalennox.com.

Books by Kara Lennox

HARLEQUIN INTRIGUE
756—BOUNTY HUNTER RANSOM†
805—BOUNTY HUNTER REDEMPTION†

HARLEQUIN AMERICAN ROMANCE
841—VIRGIN PROMISE
856—TWIN EXPECTATIONS
871—TAME AN OLDER MAN
893—BABY BY THE BOOK
917—THE UNLAWFULLY WEDDED PRINCESS
934—VIXEN IN DISGUISE*
942—PLAIN JANE'S PLAN*
951—SASSY CINDERELLA*
974—FORTUNE'S TWINS
990—THE MILLIONAIRE NEXT DOOR

†Code of the Cobra
*How To Marry a Hardison

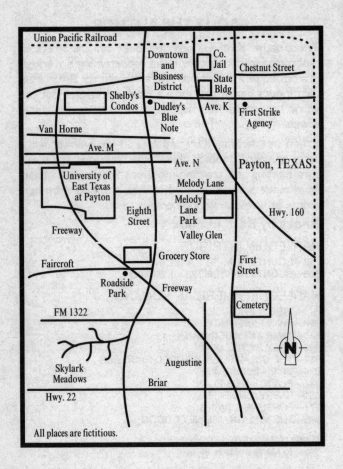

CAST OF CHARACTERS

Shelby Dorset—Someone is trying to kidnap the dedicated parole officer. Is it to get ransom from her wealthy parents, or is there a more sinister motive behind the repeated assaults?

Gavin Schuyler—The ex-con bounty hunter made some bad decisions in his past. Now he is working hard to rebuild his life. Can he protect his pretty parole officer from danger and still remain on the right side of the law?

Jake Dorset—Shelby's three-year-old son. She will do anything to keep him safe.

Rosie Amadeo—Shelby's best friend and co-worker. They've shared heartbreak and good times.

Owen Dorset—Shelby's ex-husband. He's selfish and petty, and he has a secret girlfriend. But he would never wish harm to Shelby…would he?

Manny Cruz—After a bungled kidnapping attempt, the ex-con kills himself. Was he simply unbalanced, or was someone else pulling his strings?

Paulie Sapp—The career criminal offers an implausible explanation for his attempt to kidnap Shelby.

"Rodney"—The kidnapper is known only by the name on his bogus police-uniform name tag. He claims he wants to extort money from Shelby's rich parents, but he can't keep his story straight.

Lyle Palmer—The incompetent detective seems incapable of discovering who is behind the crimes committed against Shelby, and he'd like nothing better than to see Gavin back behind bars.

Prologue

"They don't pay me enough for this," Shelby Dorset muttered as she stared down the barrel of a .38. The man holding it was just desperate enough to use it. Manny Cruz had somehow managed to slip through reception and waltz into Shelby's office full of bravado, ready to carry out the threat he'd made two weeks ago.

She hadn't worried much about the threat then. Her clients often lost their tempers when she cracked down on them. In Manny's case, he'd failed a drug test and she'd recommended to the parole board that he be returned to prison. When the guards had led him away, he'd blustered and cursed and threatened—the usual stuff. Shelby's job demanded that she mix with the lowest elements of society, some of whom naturally resented the power she held over them. No matter how fair she tried to be, no matter how equitably she tried to balance the rights of the individual against the good of society, she made some of her clients mad.

When Manny had escaped, she'd felt only slightly uneasy. Realistically, she'd figured he would run as far and as fast as he could. She'd been threatened lots of times, and nothing had ever come of it.

There was an exception to every rule, though, and the proof of that stood right in front of her.

"You're gonna stand up real easy," Manny said now. "And we're both gonna stroll right out of this office, smiling like a couple of real good friends. You got that?"

Shelby knew the decision she made now could save her life. Should she pretend to acquiesce to his demands, then alert someone as they left the office? Or should she defy him now, refuse to play the victim? Either one could get her shot.

She glanced up at the security camera above her cubicle, and a plan formed. "You'll get caught." A bead of perspiration trickled between her breasts. "It's all on tape. Security is probably watching you right now, trying to figure out how best to kill you with one shot."

Manny followed her gaze, and Shelby saw what she was hoping for—fear. She'd undermined his confidence.

Fact was, the lone security guard had a bank of two-dozen video screens to watch. He might not even notice anything was wrong. But Manny didn't know this.

Manny looked back at Shelby, his brown eyes reflecting the fear of a cornered wild animal.

"Damn you. Why couldn't you just let me alone?"

"Because—"

"Shut up! I'll tell you why. Because you enjoy messing up people's lives. You enjoy watching people squirm. You like playing God."

"But I don't—"

She didn't finish her objection. The gun went off with a deafening blast. Shelby flinched, expecting a bullet to rip into her body. But when she opened her eyes, she saw Manny Cruz slumped forward in his chair with half of his head gone.

Shelby screamed, which was wholly unnecessary, given that the moment the gun went off her cubicle was filled with half a dozen people all shouting and talking at once. Someone dragged her out from behind her desk, away from the carnage. Someone else handed her a towel. That was when she realized Manny Cruz's blood had splattered back on her. A spray of red stained her suit lapel and her white blouse—and probably her face and hair, as well.

That was when she passed out.

Chapter One

"You should give yourself more time," Shelby's friend Rosie Amadeo said as they gulped down their cappuccinos at the coffee shop on the ground floor of the State Building in downtown Payton, Texas. "I mean, my God, the guy's brains were in your hair. I'd have to stand under the shower for a week." Rosie lit a cigarette, exhaling smoke through her nose. She thoughtfully angled herself so the smoke didn't blow in Shelby's face.

"I only have forty-five minutes' worth of hot water in my water heater," Shelby said with a grimace. But she'd taken four separate showers since Manny Cruz had killed himself in her office the day before. "Anyway, I talked to the shrink. She said I could come back to work whenever I felt like it."

"She wanted you to take as much time as you needed," Rosie said. "She wasn't giving you permission to push yourself like you always do. I've never understood why you work this job anyway. Someone with your background, your connections, you could be doing anything you wanted."

"This happens to be what I want to do." Why did

everyone find that so hard to believe? She wanted to make a difference in the world, naive as that sounded. And yeah, she could have worked for some charitable foundation, distancing herself from the people she was helping. Instead, she'd chosen to use her double major in sociology and criminology to get down in the trenches with the people society had forgotten or written off. In this job, she could *see* the difference she made on a day-to-day basis.

Then there were days like yesterday.

"Shelby, you're entitled to a break. Go sit on the top of a mountain somewhere and contemplate your navel."

"I don't need more time. It's better for me to keep busy than to sit around bored."

Slowly Rosie nodded her understanding. "Owen has Jake this week?"

"Yeah." And Shelby was trying not to worry about that, either. Jake wasn't yet three years old, but already his father was finding ways to poison the child's mind against her. "Owen has a new girlfriend."

"That figures." Rosie's radar antenna focused squarely on Shelby. Nothing got Rosie jazzed more than dishing dirt. "What's she like?"

"I don't know. Owen has managed to hide her from me for weeks now—which means she's probably someone I would object to. One of his low-life clients, maybe."

"Well, Owen's a good-looking guy, even if he is a jerk," Rosie said with a shrug. "Stands to reason he wouldn't last too long without a woman in his life."

"I just wish he wouldn't expose Jake to an endless string of tarts."

Rosie blew another long stream of smoke, out the side of her mouth this time. Then she abruptly changed the subject. "So what's on your schedule today? Nothing too strenuous, I hope."

"I'm mostly out of the office. Gavin Schuyler has a new job and a new apartment. Thought I'd check those out."

Rosie gasped. "Oooooh, you are so lucky you got him. I begged Ramona, but it was your turn in the rotation, and Lord knows, Ramona won't bend the rules."

"I wish you *had* gotten him."

"Why? He's so good-looking he makes my skin itch."

"He's a cop gone bad. He stole drugs from the evidence room, then went on the lam 'cause he couldn't face up to what he did. Nothing worse in my book than someone who vows to protect the public interest, then violates the trust put in them."

"Oh, please, don't be such a self-righteous twit. He made a mistake. He paid the price. Now you get to keep him on the straight and narrow." Rosie shivered delicately. "I'd like to keep him on *my* straight and narrow."

Shelby laughed despite herself. She and Rosie had been friends since Shelby had first walked into the office, green as a new blade of grass. Rosie was foul-mouthed, plainspoken and irreverent, everything Shelby was not. She wore tight sweaters in wild colors that emphasized her enviable bustline, while Shelby wore conservative suits. But Shelby admired the way Rosie had overcome an unfortunate childhood and never dwelled on her problems. Just last year, Rosie had given birth to a stillborn child. The loss had ripped the guts out of her already shaky marriage, and her husband had left. But she certainly didn't sit around feeling sorry for herself.

Shelby intended to follow Rosie's example. No whining, no endless ruminating on how she might have prevented Manny's suicide. She had to get on with her life.

As Shelby pulled her silver Volvo into a parking place on Avenue K, she dragged her thoughts to the case at hand.

She didn't get out of the car right away. She wanted to get a feel for who was going in and out of the First Strike Agency, Gavin Schuyler's new place of employment.

She'd nearly hit the roof when he'd told her he wanted to work with bounty hunters. But when he'd explained what his duties would be—and that Beau Maddox would be training him and keeping an eye on him—she had reserved judgment. He would be doing investigative work, like skip tracing and surveillance, for which he was eminently qualified as a former police detective. But he wouldn't participate in takedowns. He claimed he wouldn't have any personal contact with criminal elements or ever go near a gun.

She'd checked around. First Strike had an unsavory image—probably one it promoted—but a good reputation, at least as far as its success record. Her office had actually worked with the agency to bring in parolees who had cut and run, and First Strike almost always found their targets and brought them back into the system without bloodshed.

Still, Shelby had a niggling sensation that she needed to check things out personally. And she definitely wanted to see Gavin's new living quarters. Along with a job, Ace McCullough, First Strike's owner, had offered Gavin the loft above the office at an unbelievably cheap rent. She had no problem with Gavin leaving the halfway house where he'd been since his release from Huntsville back in August. She believed he was ready to make it on his own. But the transition to full independence could be tricky, and she wanted to keep an extra close eye on him until she was sure he'd adjusted.

Her initial impression of First Strike was hardly encouraging. The agency was housed in a strip shopping center between a pawnshop and a bail bondsman, in a part of town where she wouldn't dare walk after dark.

Faded white lettering on a tattered blue awning above the door identified the place, along with a picture of a coiled cobra, ready to strike. The barred windows were so filthy she could see nothing inside.

No one came in or out during the ten minutes Shelby spent watching the place. She imagined they didn't get a lot of walk-in traffic, though. So she opened her door and stepped out into the chilly November morning, then mentally braced herself for another encounter with the sexiest man she'd ever met.

She downplayed Gavin's obvious physical attributes whenever his name came up at the office, pretending she was indifferent to the primal male sexuality that practically wafted off his body. But he did more than make her skin itch.

Shelby did not consider this a good thing.

"WHEN DO YOU THINK he'll be back?" Gavin asked politely over the phone, his adrenaline surging. *Yes.* He'd located Desmond Fiche less than twenty-four hours after he'd been given the case, his first as an employee of First Strike.

Tracking down a bail jumper wasn't quite the same

as being a real detective with a badge and a gun. But that was one dream Gavin would have to let go of. He would never, ever wear a badge again, and that was a fact of life. He'd forfeited that privilege when he'd broken the law in such spectacular fashion.

He hadn't set out to be a criminal. He'd been working undercover, determined to bring some drug dealers to justice. But he'd immersed himself a little too deeply in his role, and there came a point when he had to either use drugs—strictly against the rules—or blow his cover. He'd smoked crack, thinking he could handle it. But he'd quickly become addicted. And instead of owning up to his mistake, he tried to hide it as the addiction gradually overwhelmed him.

He'd gotten away with it, the first two times he'd stolen drugs from the evidence room. The third time, he'd gotten caught. And that was the end of his law-enforcement career. And the beginning of his salvation. Because being free of the curse of addiction was worth any price.

But being a bounty hunter might be almost as good as being a cop. At least he could use his brain again, match wits with a scumbag who thought he was smarter than the system. He'd still be getting criminals off the street.

Ironically, it was a bounty hunter from this very agency who'd brought Gavin in when he'd gone on the lam. Beau Maddox, his best friend from childhood, could have shot his head off and been perfectly within his legal rights. Fortunately for Gavin, Beau had shot him in the leg instead. That was all it had taken to make Gavin see what an idiot he'd been.

That, and two-plus years in the state lockup in Huntsville.

"I really need to talk to Des," Gavin said. "I used to work with him. He's got another paycheck coming, and we don't know where to send it."

Gavin held his breath. This ploy almost always worked. He grinned when the receptionist took his bait. "I can give you his address."

"That'd be super." He jotted down the street address, thanked the receptionist and hung up.

That was when he saw her. Shelby Dorset, his parole officer, standing in the middle of the office, taking it all in.

Oh, holy hell. What was she doing here? Why hadn't he heard the door open? She'd made some vague comment last week about wanting to check out his new job, but she hadn't said anything about coming today.

She just stood there, looking as if she was in the Chamber of Horrors. And in a way, she was. For a bunch of guys, the First Strike office was comfortably lived-in. But a classy woman like Shelby would consider this place a living nightmare.

He tried to see it through her eyes.

All right, so the place wasn't much to look at. Battered wooden desks, all of which looked as if they'd been rescued from a scrap heap, were arranged haphazardly around the deep, narrow main room. Every available surface was cluttered with papers, folders, dirty coffee mugs and—oh, God—empty beer bottles.

In one corner was a home gym—a weight bench and a couple of machines with torn, blue-sparkle vinyl upholstery. Dingy towels, stiff with sweat, hung from various bars on the workout machine, and—was that a jockstrap?

Oh, terrific.

The floor was partially covered with faded blue indoor-outdoor carpeting. The carpet had great, gaping holes and rips, through which a bare concrete floor shone.

The walls were dingy white. Someone had made a half-hearted attempt to paint in the not-too-distant past, but it looked as though his or her efforts had ended before the first can of paint had.

An army-green plastic garbage can sat in the center of the room, overflowing with beer bottles, fast-food containers and empty ammo boxes. That looked bad, especially when Gavin had made a point to emphasize he would not go near any weapons. Shelby would probably think they all took target practice in the parking lot out back.

And speaking of target practice, one entire wall was covered with Wanted posters, darts protruding from the mug shots.

The acoustic tiles on the ceiling—the ones that weren't missing—were stained and crumbling, and the flickering fluorescent light fixtures, caked with decades of dust, bathed the entire mess in surreal bluish light.

He was sunk.

Shelby's delicate, aristocratic nose wrinkled slightly at the smell of sweat and stale pizza that permeated the office. She suddenly turned her laserlike gaze toward Gavin. "Good morning."

Gavin shot out of his chair so abruptly it rolled backward and hit the wall behind him. "Morning, Ms. Dorset." He resisted the urge to add "ma'am." Something about Shelby made him think of his fifth-grade teacher, Mrs. Applebaum. Who, come to think of it, was the object of his first sexual fantasy. Prim-and-proper good girls always flipped his switch. "I didn't know you were coming today."

"I had planned to give you a little more time to settle in," she said. "But they're, uh, doing some work on my office today." She paused, cleared her throat, looked away. That was odd. He'd never seen her less than one hundred percent assured. "I needed to get out."

The back door of the office opened, and Ace and Lori entered, apparently in the midst of one of their frequent, animated arguments. Ace McCullough owned First Strike. A Vietnam vet in his late fifties, he was also an ex-con. But, like Gavin, he'd served his time when he was young and had apparently learned his lesson, because he'd stayed out of serious trouble for twenty-five years despite his slightly rakish image. He'd started the agency when Judge Glenn Bettencourt, weary of the justice system's revolving door for criminals, had decided on a career change and had asked Ace, an old war buddy, to join him.

Glenn had been murdered eighteen months ago. Lori was his daughter. She had bounty hunting in her blood, but her father had never allowed her to join the agency. Now that he wasn't around to object, here she was. Ace had taken her under his wing, figuring if she was determined to be a bounty hunter, she might as well get trained by the best.

"There was no need to throw me onto the ground," the slender, athletic-looking blonde groused as she pulled her camouflage sweatshirt over her head, revealing the Kevlar vest she wore underneath. "Like I don't have enough sense to find cover when someone starts shooting?"

Lori's gun, which she wore tucked into the back of her black hip-hugger jeans, was plainly visible.

Great. Perfect timing.

Shelby just watched the newcomers, seemingly fascinated.

"Ace? Lori?" Gavin called out, because they were so engrossed in their argument they didn't realize a stranger was in their midst. Both stopped talking and looked at Gavin, then at Shelby. "This is Shelby Dorset, my parole officer."

Lori and Ace immediately grasped the significance. Lori slapped her hand over her mouth, probably to prevent herself from saying something else that would hammer another nail into Gavin's coffin. Ace, though, came forward, hand outstretched, his best welcoming smile in place.

"How do you do, Ms. Dorset?" he said graciously. "Lori, why don't you make us all some coffee?"

Even Gavin knew that was the wrong thing to say to Lori. It had taken less than a day for him to figure out Lori had a chip on her shoulder about being the only woman working here. It was bad enough she got stuck doing the bulk of the secretarial work, she'd told Gavin, but she positively refused to clean up after the other slobs who worked here—or play waitress.

Ace was taking a big risk, asking her to make coffee.

Lori took a breath, a vociferous objection ready to erupt.

"I'll make coffee," Gavin said quickly. He nodded to Shelby as he passed her. If anyone could convince the prissy parole officer that First Strike was a healthful, nurturing environment for a man striving to integrate back into society, it was Ace. He had a line of bull for any occasion. A trained hostage negotiator, he'd once talked a crazed gunman into a peaceful surrender in five minutes flat, and the gunman had thanked Ace profusely as he was led away in handcuffs.

As Gavin passed Lori, he whispered, "Get rid of the gun."

She gave another little gasp.

The agency's coffeemaker was a giant, restaurant-grade machine, another junkyard find. Rex Bettencourt, Lori's brother and another of First Strike's bounty hunters, had repaired it and turned it into something that produced the blackest, strongest and most potent brew outside of a tar pit. Gavin had met Rex only briefly, at Beau's wedding a couple of months ago. But after some of the stories the others had told him, he looked forward to watching the ex-marine work. He was somewhere out west this week, tracking down a church bomber with a quarter-million-dollar price on his head.

Lori joined Gavin in the kitchenette, her sweatshirt back on. "Think we can find a clean cup around here?"

"I'll have to wash something." He selected a plain white mug from the pile of dirty dishes in the sink and ran some scalding water and a little dish soap into a plastic dishpan.

"I'm really sorry, Gavin," Lori blurted out. "I hope Ace and I didn't ruin things for you with our Rambo talk and weapons display." Since the soapy water was there, she started washing the other dishes. "I locked my gun up in the safe, and I made sure your friend saw me do it. What's the story with her, anyway? She looks like she ought to be sipping tea with her sorority sisters, not running around bad neighborhoods checking up on ex-cons. Oh, sorry."

"No offense taken. It's what I am. As for Shelby, I haven't even begun to figure her out."

She was one of the most beautiful women he'd ever encountered, with a body-made-for-sin encased in a never-ending array of schoolmarm suits. Her artfully streaked blond hair was always pulled into a tightly controlled twist, not a pin out of place. Her makeup was flawless, though she downplayed her huge blue eyes and pouty lips with muted colors. Her jewelry, when she wore any, was understated, but he knew it was expensive just the same.

Her one concession to vampiness was her shoes. Most of the state-government employees he'd encountered wore low heels or serviceable flats. But Shelby Dorset always had on a pair of three-inch spikes, expensive-looking shoes made of what looked like suede or kid or eel skin in a rainbow of designer colors. He'd never seen the same pair twice.

Though Shelby's skirts were of a modest length, those high heels made her legs a sight to behold.

The moment he'd met Shelby, his heart had raced and his palms had grown damp, and various other parts of his anatomy had stirred with interest. Her voice, husky, slow, yet refined, had skittered along his spine like a feather duster.

He tried to tell himself he'd been too long without a woman. Maybe so, but none of the other females he saw made his mouth go dry. His biggest challenge during their biweekly meetings was to not let Shelby know how hot she made him. Because he was sure any hint of impropriety would lead him right back to the big house.

"Is she at least reasonable?" Lori asked. "First impressions aside, this is a good place for you to work. We're kind of like a family. We look out for each other. Ace is a stickler for following rules. I mean, he protects me as if I was his own daughter. Sometimes he protects me a little too much, in fact."

Gavin knew this was the place he belonged. He'd felt it the first hour of the first day. Beau and Ace and Lori had gone out of their way to make him feel like one of the gang. And the work—it challenged his mind and made him feel like a human being with something to contribute. For the first time since his arrest three years ago, he was starting to think he could bounce back from the colossal mistake he'd made.

His life would never be the same, but it might still be worth living.

Miraculously, Lori found a tray. She filled four mugs with coffee while Gavin found some packets of powdered creamer and sugar. He had to beat the sugar packets with a hammer to break them up, but they looked okay. There were no napkins in the kitchenette; paper towels would have to do. Paper towels with little blue ducks.

Back in the main room, Ace was showing Shelby "The Gallery." That was a special section of mug shots belonging to fugitives the First Strike bounty hunters had actually apprehended and collected rewards on. Gavin quietly groaned. He knew Ace was proud that he and his associates had taken some dangerous characters off the street. But he didn't think this was something that ought to be emphasized to Shelby.

Gavin pushed some beer bottles out of the way and set the coffee tray down on one of the desks. His heart

skipped a beat when he noticed a pile of magazines—
Soldier of Fortune, Guns & Ammo and *Playboy*—which
he casually stuffed into a drawer. Not that Shelby hadn't
already seen them. Her sharp blue eyes didn't look as
though they missed many details.

Ace looked at the tray, then at Gavin and Lori. Gavin
could tell he was trying not to laugh. The gesture
seemed so ridiculous now, they might as well have
brought out a china tea set.

"Coffee, Ms. Dorset?" Gavin asked.

"Thank you, but I…better not." She paused, then
looked at him standing there like a dodo next to the tray.
"I guess I should have said something before you went
to all this trouble."

"I sterilized the cup," he said. Ace and Lori stared at
him, and he realized he'd said something aloud that he'd
only intended to think. Shelby actually cracked a smile.

"It's not that I don't want the coffee. But I've already
had my one cup for the day. More than that makes me
jumpy."

Wow. Had the woman actually volunteered some information about herself?

"So, Gavin, why don't you show me what kind of
work you're doing?"

He took Shelby over to the reception desk, which was
his "office" for the moment. Low man on the totem
pole had to answer the phone at First Strike, he explained. But when he showed her the stack of files he
was working on, tracking down fugitives, missing children, deadbeats, he forgot about trying to gain Shelby's
approval and got enthusiastic about his job.

He explained the various techniques he used, simply

by employing the telephone, to glean information. If his information led to an apprehension, he shared in the bounty. And until he got up to speed, Ace would pay him a small stipend to cover his very modest expenses and allow him to live in the loft at a reduced rent, provided he cleaned it out and made some improvements.

"Why don't we take a look at that loft?" Shelby asked.

Gavin had been dreading that suggestion. "It's still kind of a mess. I haven't had much time to—"

"That's all right. I just need to ascertain that it's up to code and includes the basics."

Therein lay the problem. With a sigh, he led Shelby through the storage room, out the back door and up a rickety set of metal stairs. He unlocked three dead bolts—it was a bad neighborhood, after all—and opened the door to allow her to enter.

The loft was actually huge, including the space above First Strike as well as the two offices on either side. It had tremendous potential, with solid pine-plank floor-ing, exposed brick walls and twelve-foot ceilings. Un-fortunately, it was filled to the rafters with trash—old furniture, moldering boxes of God-knew-what, stacks of ancient newspapers, a pile of industrial light fixtures circa 1960, broken electronic equipment.

"Oh, my," was all Shelby could manage.

"I'll have to get a truck and haul all this stuff to the landfill," Gavin explained. "I just haven't had time yet."

Shelby picked her way over to Gavin's "bedroom," which consisted of a pallet on a piece of floor he'd cleared out, and a suitcase with his meager supply of clothes—everything that hadn't been stolen from him at the halfway house. His sister, Aubrey—now Beau's wife—had sold everything else he owned to help pay for his legal defense.

"Where's the bathroom?"

"Um, Ms. Dorset, you don't want to go in there." The bathroom had a working toilet, but that was it. No sink, no tub or shower, no towel racks, and no light. "When Rex Bettencourt gets back from out of town later in the week—he's Lori's brother, and he works here, too— he's going to help me put in a real bathroom, with a shower and lights and everything. Meanwhile, I shower at the Y down the street," he admitted. "But like I said, just temporary."

"Kitchen?"

Gavin shook his head. "I don't cook."

"What do you eat? I know the halfway house wasn't ideal, but at least they provided one solid meal every day."

"The deli around the corner has fresh sandwiches. Look, Ms. Dorset—"

"You can call me Shelby, you know. We've gotten to know each other pretty well over the past few months, don't you think?"

It was on the tip of his tongue to say, "Lady, you don't know the first thing about me, and you've revealed absolutely nothing of yourself except that too much caffeine makes you nervous." But he bit his tongue, because his smart mouth had been getting him into trouble since kindergarten, and trouble was one thing he was determined to avoid.

"My mama taught me that first names were too familiar when dealing with authority figures, ma'am," he said instead.

He could tell his obsequious reply made her mad, and

he took some satisfaction in that. Hell, this meeting was in the garbage, anyway. Nothing to lose.

"I don't like to think of myself as an authority figure," she said. "I like to think of us as teammates, working together to integrate you back into society and coming up with strategies to avoid repeating past mistakes. I like to think that I'm a help, rather than a hindrance, to your rising to your full potential."

"Begging your pardon, ma'am, but when one person has the power to send the other one to jail, that's an authority figure in my book." The more barriers he kept between himself and his long-legged parole officer, the better chance he had at stopping before he made a fool of himself. He could go crazy just watching her walk or listening to the soft purr of her voice.

"Then we'll keep things as they are," she said, but he could tell she didn't like it that he'd rebuffed her attempt to bond.

"I know this place looks bad," he said. "But for the first time in three years, I can sleep through the night without worrying about whether someone's going to empty out my wallet during the night—or slip a knife between my ribs. Don't make me go back to the halfway house. Give me a week."

Shelby was silent a moment. Finally she said, "Believe it or not, Gavin, I'm not unreasonable. While the physical environments here and at your office aren't ideal, I worry much more about the people you surround yourself with. I like Ace and Lori, despite their rough edges. And I know Beau Maddox by reputation, at least.

"More importantly, I can see you like it here. You were actually smiling when you told me about your work, and I haven't seen you smile before, ever. So I'm going to approve your new situation, on the condition you bring the apartment up to code. And you better do it fast, before the city finds you and evicts you."

Surprise and relief flooded through Gavin's body. "Thank you, Ms. Dorset."

"I'll give you a couple of weeks before I visit again, okay?"

Damn, maybe she really was a human being. He felt a tremendous urge to throw his arms around her in gratitude…or maybe something else. He settled for a handshake.

"You got a deal."

A zing of awareness shot through his arm, then his body, when he touched her. He worked to control the shudder of awareness, but he was acutely sensitive to the chamois-soft texture of her skin. Her light scent suddenly reminded him of standing in a peach orchard on a summer day. He shook his head to clear it of such ridiculous images.

They went back downstairs and through the offices, where all four cups of coffee still sat on the tray, untouched and growing cold. Ace was on the phone and Lori had her head stuck in a filing cabinet, but they both waved and smiled as Shelby made her way toward the front door.

She paused at the home gym to stare at the jockstrap. "Nice touch. Who's your decorator?"

Gavin had no reply to that. What could he say? At least Shelby had a sense of humor.

He walked her to the door, then watched through the barred window as she pushed a button on her key chain to unlock the doors on her silver Volvo. It was a nice car, pretty new, immaculate, of course. He wondered how she afforded her car and her clothes and especially her shoes on a chintzy government salary.

Then he realized that was a stupid question. She had a rich husband, probably. She didn't wear a wedding ring, but maybe it was a big ol' rock of a diamond that she didn't feel comfortable flashing in front of her parolees.

She slid behind the wheel, swung her elegant legs inside the car. Just for a second, her skirt shifted, letting him see past those great calves and all the way up to slender muscled thighs. Just the way he liked them. He exhaled sharply as she closed the door, then kept watching as she started the engine, checked the rearview mirror and slowly backed the car into the street.

That was when he realized she wasn't alone in the car. A figure rose up from the back seat.

He watched in frozen horror for a split second. Then he went into action. "Ace! Lori! A man just pulled a gun on Shelby!"

Chapter Two

The man had one hand at Shelby's throat, his meaty fingers wrapped around her chin to keep her head facing forward. The other hand held a gun, its muzzle pressing in just under her jaw.

She glanced at him in the rearview mirror. White, midthirties, with a dark crew cut. Not at all familiar.

"Do exactly as I say," he growled, his bad breath nearly choking her, "and no one will get hurt. Now put it in Drive and go forward, toward the highway."

This couldn't be happening, Shelby thought dazedly. Held at gunpoint two days in a row?

God, how had she let this scum get the best of her? How could she have climbed into her car without checking the back seat?

More to the point, how was she going to get out of this? Never let a bad guy take you to a second location. She knew that advice by heart. If someone pulled a gun or knife on you and tried to get you into a vehicle, you were supposed to fight right then and never assume you would have a better chance to escape later. Because once a guy had you in a car, he could take you to some secluded spot and dispose of you at his leisure. Well, she'd messed up on rule number one. She was in a car with him. Was there a number two?

Still, she had some advantages here, she thought, ordering herself to think clearly as she changed gears and put light pressure on the gas pedal. She was behind the wheel. She was still in a relatively populated area, near businesses and cars, though she didn't actually see anyone on the street.

She could jerk the steering wheel and wreck the car. But that would work better if she had witnesses who would come running to help, or at least call the police. She could slam on the brakes and try to get out of the car. But the scumbag had a good grip on her. Her chances of getting away were slim.

"If you're thinking about having an accident, don't," he said. "We've got Jake, so you better cooperate."

Ice water surged through Shelby's veins. Her baby, her Jake. She forced herself not to panic. "Where is he?"

"Safe enough for the time being."

"What do you want?" She was driving haphazardly down the street. Her abductor hadn't given her specific instructions.

"Turn right at the light."

The light was where Avenue K intersected Highway 160. He wanted her to head out of town. Not a good sign.

She pressed on the brake, amazed she could summon the coordination to continue driving. "Look, if it's money you want—"

"Shut up. Turn."

That was when Shelby saw the black Blazer in the rearview mirror. Oh, God, oh, no. It was Ace McCullough behind the wheel, and Lori in the passenger seat. Had they witnessed her abduction?

The Blazer honked.

"What the—?" The scumbag turned his head to look out the back window.

"They're bounty hunters," Shelby said evenly. "I was parked outside their office. They probably saw you pull the gun on me."

"Keep driving." The scumbag sounded scared now. Panicked, even. Memories of Manny Cruz's look of fear intruded into Shelby's chaotic thoughts.

Reminding Manny that he was going to be caught had only produced panic and bloodshed. She wouldn't make the same mistake with this guy.

"Listen to me," she said. "I want to cooperate with you. I'll do anything you want as long as you don't hurt my son. But if I don't pull over and tell these guys I'm okay and you're an old friend with a really bad idea of a practical joke, they're not going away. They might even kill you."

The kidnapper held on to her even more tightly. "They won't shoot me, not when I'm this close to you."

"You don't know these guys."

The Blazer honked at them again.

"Drive. Do what I say. We'll ditch 'em."

"A Volvo can't outrun a Blazer," she reasoned.

"Shut up!" His voice had gained an octave.

The guy was losing it. She knew the bounty hunters were doing what they thought was the right thing, coming to her rescue. But the added pressure of a chase was liable to flip this guy's switch from nervous to full panic. Still, what else could they have done? Let her drive off with a gun pointed at her head? They didn't know about Jake, or that she would rather risk herself than put her precious child in harm's way.

She was on the two-lane highway now, accelerating, the Blazer on her bumper. She opened the window. "I'm going to wave them past."

"Okay. Do it."

She slowed down, then stuck her arm out the window and gestured as though she wanted them to pass.

The Blazer accelerated and pulled into the oncoming lane, and for a moment she thought her ploy was actually going to work. Fortunately, the highway wasn't heavily trafficked this time of day.

But the Blazer didn't pass. It drove alongside her, matching her pace. The Blazer's passenger window slid open to reveal Lori pointing a gun at Shelby's car.

"Pull over, Ms. Dorset!"

"Don't do it!" the thug screamed in her ear. "Or I'll kill you right here! Then I'll kill Jake."

Shelby was paralyzed with indecision. She simply had no idea what to do.

"Your chances for survival are better if you *pull over!*" Lori screamed. "I don't want to shoot your tires out, but I will if I have to."

"You even slow down," her attacker growled in her ear, "your brains will be spattered all over this car."

"He'll hurt my baby!" Shelby screamed back at Lori. "Please, back off!"

That was when she heard glass shattering. Oh, God, was someone shooting? Then she realized that a pair of cowboy boots had just burst through the window behind her and into the back seat, knocking her abductor away from her. Abruptly the thug lost his grip on her head. The gun no longer pressed into her jaw.

She didn't dare slam on the brakes now, or she might bisect the man who was half in her car, half still in the Blazer. That man, she realized, could be none other than Gavin Schuyler.

A deafening blast nearly burst Shelby's eardrums as a gun detonated in her enclosed car. Her windshield shattered. Bits of glass blew back into her face, her eyes. She had to stop, or she risked having a head-on collision with someone coming from the other direction.

As she slowed the car, she realized Gavin was still struggling with the thug behind her. There was a lot of yelling and cursing, and the sound of sickening, bone-crushing thuds as blows were exchanged.

The moment her car came to a stop, the driver's door jerked open, a hand unfastened her seat belt, and she was unceremoniously dragged from the car and dumped onto the pavement.

"Get down!" It was Lori.

Sprawled on her back, with small rocks digging into her hips and shoulders, Shelby still couldn't see. She heard more car doors opening, and finally, "Okay, it's over, we got him."

Shelby should have felt relief she was safe. But anger welled up inside her at the high-handed manner in which the bounty hunters had "saved" her. They had put her at risk; worse, they'd endangered her son.

Gentle hands held Shelby down as she tried to lift herself off the pavement. "Ms. Dorset?" It was Gavin. "Don't try to move. You're injured."

She could feel blood trickling down her cheek toward

her ear. "Got glass in my face," she said. But as she blinked a few times, she realized her tears had already washed out the tiny specks of safety glass from her eyes. She could see, and she wasn't otherwise seriously injured. "Let me up. I need my phone."

"We've already called the police and an ambulance."

Finally she could focus on Gavin's face, staring down into hers with concern. He was on one knee beside her, one hand on her shoulder to keep her down.

"He said he had my son," Shelby said, knowing it was imperative that she remain calm to get her message across. "He said he would hurt my baby if I didn't cooperate."

"Where is your son supposed to be right now?" A new urgency had entered Gavin's voice.

"At day care."

"I'll get your phone." He let her go. She took the opportunity to sit up and assess her condition for herself. She didn't see any bullet holes or blood beyond what came from a scraped knee; her hose were shot, but all of her limbs appeared to be intact.

She wanted to stand, to jump to her feet and find her phone, but her body simply would not obey the commands she gave it. She was probably in mild shock, and who wouldn't be? She leaned back against the front tire of her car, limp as a stalk of old celery.

Gavin reappeared moments later with her red suede purse. "Is the phone in here?"

She nodded and took the purse, reached in and came up with her cell phone. The number for the church daycare center where either she or Owen took Jake every day was preprogrammed into her phone. She dialed it.

"Sunshine Day Care."

"Susan, this is Shelby Dorset. Is Jake there?"

"You want to speak to him?" Susan sounded a bit bewildered by Shelby's urgent tone.

"Just tell me—is he there right now? Can you see him?"

"Just a minute." There was a pause that seemed interminable, but was probably only a few seconds. "Yes, Ms. Dorset, I can see him. He's in the story group right now."

Shelby took the first full breath she'd allowed herself since the man had taken her prisoner. "I know this is a strange request, but I would like to talk to him. I just need to say hi."

"Okay," Susan said cheerfully. "Don't worry, children aren't the only ones to suffer separation anxiety. I get calls like this all the time."

Moments later, Shelby heard Jake's childish, "Hi, Mommy!" And she could finally, once and for all, believe he was safe. She spoke to him for a minute, then got Susan on the line.

"I can't go into details," Shelby said, "but I've been assaulted and Jake was threatened. So please keep a very close watch on him until either his father or I can pick him up."

GAVIN LISTENED to the one-sided conversation, never taking his gaze off Shelby. She had a child? He'd never thought of her in those terms.

He gathered from the look on her face that her son was okay. "We can send—the police can send someone over to check on him, if you want," he said, wanting to reassure her. For a minute there, he'd forgotten that he was no longer with the police himself. The chase, the rescue, the takedown, all had catapulted him back in time to his days as a cop.

"That would be good." She sounded as though she was fighting tears. But of course she wouldn't want her parolee to see her crying.

"Do you know the man who abducted you?" Gavin asked, still in cop mode.

"I only saw him in the mirror. He was behind me the whole time. But he didn't seem at all familiar. How did he even know I had a son?"

"Maybe it was a lucky guess. Most women in your age range do have young children. He would have been looking for something to use as leverage, to gain your cooperation."

Shelby shook her head. "He said Jake's name."

Gavin felt a compulsion to touch her, to comfort her. Though he knew she was tall for a woman, right now she looked so small, scared and vulnerable. He settled for picking a couple of leaves and twigs off her suit jacket, then one out of her hair, which had come loose from its normally tightly controlled twist. It hung to her shoulders, silky soft and almost straight, the blond high-lights glistening in the sun.

"You're safe now, and so's Jake. It's all over."

Gavin expected Shelby to at least thank him for sav-ing her life. He could have gotten killed himself with that Indiana Jones maneuver, vaulting out of a moving vehicle, kicking through a window and launching him-self feetfirst at a guy with a gun. His leg throbbed with pain, and he had to struggle not to limp. The old bullet wound usually didn't hurt unless he abused it. Right now, it felt as if someone was stabbing him in the thigh with a butcher knife.

But Shelby didn't look particularly grateful, and she probably wouldn't be sympathetic to his pain. In fact, she seemed a bit testy.

"You could have gotten me killed with that stunt of yours."

"Excuse me?" Definitely testy.

"He had a gun to my head. There were a dozen ways you could have handled it when you realized I was being kidnapped. You could have called the cops and given them a description of my—"

"Begging your pardon, ma'am, but if he'd gotten you out of our sight, he'd have taken you down some country road where no one could spot you, and you'd be dead right now. Or you'd be tied up and tortured, raped, then murdered."

She paled at his words, and he felt a pang of guilt for describing her alternate fate so graphically. But, damn it, he'd been a cop for a lot of years. He knew what he was talking about. The fact she thought he'd taken unnecessary risks irked him.

"I bet he told you you wouldn't get hurt if you cooperated, right?" he asked.

She nodded. "You could have followed at a discreet distance."

"To what end?"

"So you wouldn't panic him. The last guy with a gun who panicked around me shot his own head off."

That shut down Gavin's next argument. He'd read about the suicide at the State Building in this morning's paper. But the news account had been sketchy as to which office, exactly, the death had occurred in. He'd had no idea the shooter had been threatening a parole officer, much less that it had been Shelby.

He recalled Shelby's comment earlier about needing to get out of the office while they did some work, and how her voice had shaken.

"I'd have talked him out of hurting me," Shelby said. "If you guys hadn't rushed in like a herd of Rambos…"

He wasn't going to argue with her. He and Ace and Lori had taken a calculated risk by going on the offensive so quickly. Yes, there'd been a very real possibility the guy would shoot Shelby. But every moment they allowed the perp to keep Shelby under his power was another moment she was in danger. The longer he had her, the stronger his control would have been over her.

They'd have had to confront Shelby's abductor at some point. Gavin didn't believe the danger to Shelby would have been any less had they waited. Better to take down the perp while he was still off balance.

Lori came over, and Gavin forced himself to stand and walk away from Shelby. He'd done his part. She didn't need him now, obviously didn't want his comfort or his reassurances. And she definitely didn't want to claim him as her hero.

Gavin was embarrassed to admit that he'd been hoping for that very thing.

LORI HANDED SHELBY a wad of paper towels. "You okay?"

"I'm not hurt. Just shaky." Which was exactly what she'd said yesterday when one of her co-workers had tried to help her wipe Manny Cruz's blood off her face. Just before she'd passed out.

She'd never fainted in her life until yesterday. But here she was, scarcely twenty-four hours later, weak and shaky again.

Lori reached into the side pocket of her khaki cargo pants and produced an energy bar. "Here. Your blood sugar is probably in the basement."

Shelby didn't really want to eat, but Lori's gesture was so kind, she felt obligated. "Thanks." She unwrapped the bar and nibbled on it.

"Sorry I yelled at you earlier," Lori said.

"I'm sorry I didn't listen. But he said he'd kill me if I slowed down."

"Not to overdramatize, but he was going to kill you anyway."

"That's what Gavin said."

"Well, he was right." Lori paused, then asked, "Is he going to be in trouble because of this?"

"Gavin? No," Shelby said quietly. But approaching sirens reminded her that she wasn't the only one who could cause trouble for Gavin. The police would have to do a thorough investigation of this incident. And the Payton Police Department was notoriously hard on civilians doing the vigilante thing.

Shelby ate a few more bites of the energy bar. Amazingly, she felt a little better. She wasn't quite as numb now. In fact, she was sentient enough to notice the chill November wind whistling through her thin suit jacket.

"Do you want a blanket?" Lori asked.

"Actually, I'd like to get up off this cold, hard ground."

"Why don't you wait 'til the paramedics check you out?"

Shelby shook her head. "I'm not hurt. I have a few little scratches on my face from flying glass." To prove her point, she pushed herself up to a partial squat, then winced when she saw her knee. She'd scraped them when she'd fallen out of the car. But she persevered, and pretty soon she was actually standing.

The heel on one of her Prada red-suede pumps had broken off. Damn, it was her favorite pair, too. She knew it was silly of her to worry about something so trivial as a shoe when she'd almost been killed. But maybe it was easier to focus on the trivial than think too hard about what had almost happened.

She didn't want Jake to grow up without a mother.

A patrol car pulled up, lights flashing, and two uniforms got out. Ace, who seemed to be the one in charge of their little situation now, swaggered up to the cops and started talking. But they sidestepped him and came straight to her.

"Ms. Dorset." One of them, a tall, lanky farm-boy type with strawberry-blond hair, offered a wry smile. His name tag identified him as Perkins. "You're having a bad week."

That was an understatement.

Two hours later, Shelby sat in an interview room at the police station, waiting for some detective to show up and question her about her kidnapping. She was hungry, cranky, and she had a headache.

She had Jake with her, and he was even more fussy than Shelby was. When Perkins had wanted to drive her to the police station for more questioning, she'd insisted on stopping at the day-care center first. So long as she had Jake's warm, sturdy little body in her arms, she could stand the rest of this ordeal.

Her cell phone chimed and she answered, grateful to have a diversion. It was Owen.

"What the hell is going on?" he demanded without preamble. "What do you think you're doing, taking Jake when it's not your week?"

Typical. Owen would of course be more concerned with following the rules of their hotly debated custody arrangements than with her safety, or even Jake's. "I'll deliver him to you the moment you're home from work," she said. "You won't miss any time with him. But you were in court, and I couldn't just leave him at the day-care center. Oh, Owen, I was kidnapped, and this awful man said he would hurt Jake."

"You were—*what?*"

"This man hid in my car and pointed a gun at me. He had very bad intentions, I'm afraid."

"I don't know why you keep working at that terrible job!" Owen exploded. "It's not like you need the money. Now not only are you putting yourself in danger, but you're endangering my son."

"Yes, I'm fine, thanks for your concern," Shelby said tightly.

Silence. Then, "Okay, sorry. *Are* you okay?"

"Just some bruises and scratches."

"And Jake?"

"Jake is fine."

As if to prove the point, Jake grabbed the phone from Shelby. "Daddy? Daddy?"

Shelby allowed Jake to babble to Owen for a minute, then took the phone back.

Owen continued the conversation as if there'd never been a break. "Mark my words, this crime is connected to your job somehow."

"As far as I know, the kidnapper wasn't one of my parolees," Shelby pointed out. "In fact, one of the guys I supervise saved me."

"I still don't think you should expose yourself to all those criminals. Something like this was bound to happen sooner or later."

"And your job *doesn't* expose you to criminals?" Owen got most of his clients by trolling police stations and checking the arrest blotter. He also got work as a court-appointed attorney for suspects who couldn't afford to hire a lawyer.

Hardly an elite client list.

"That's different. I'm a man, I can take care of myself."

This was a familiar argument, one Shelby didn't want to revisit.

The door to the interview room opened. "Listen, I have to go. Just call me on my cell when you're on your way home. I'll drop Jake off at your house or meet you anywhere you say." Of course, she didn't have a car. She would have to figure something out.

"All right. Shelby…sorry about yelling. I was just shocked and upset at what you told me. I really am relieved you're okay. Tell Jakey I'll see him soon."

Shelby ended the conversation as a detective entered the interview room. She was appalled to realize she recognized him. In fact, they'd served together on a crime-prevention task force a couple of years ago. What she remembered about Lyle Palmer was that he was a brownnosing, pontificating, not-too-bright guy who'd obviously been promoted to detective by mistake. She suspected he'd volunteered for the task force because he liked to see his name in the newspaper. He hadn't offered up a single useful idea, but he'd been more than eager to claim others' ideas as his own if a reporter was within hearing.

This was the guy in charge of investigating her kidnapping? But she shouldn't be surprised. Somehow, Palmer always managed to get assigned to high-profile cases—which this one was, she realized. The crime rate had risen in Payton as the population had burgeoned. Even so, an aggravated kidnapping combined with an action-hero rescue would make the front page of the local paper.

"Does the name Paulie Sapp ring a bell?" Lyle asked her without preamble.

Shelby thought for a moment. "No, I can't say it does."

"He says you were his parole officer several years ago."

"Really?" Granted, she'd handled hundreds of cases over the years. But she had a pretty good memory for the men and women she supervised. Neither Paulie's name, nor his face, rang any bells.

"He says you were a real ball breaker, and he hated your guts. He just got out of prison—for the third time—and decided he was going to take what he thought he deserved. He knew your family had money, and he was going to hold you for ransom."

"So he wasn't going to kill me?"

Lyle shrugged. "No guarantees. But your bounty-hunter friends were overzealous. They could have gotten you killed. Schuyler's a former cop. He should have had better judgment."

And that's what it came down to—judgment. Every law-enforcement person handled an iffy situation a little bit differently. Maybe her "bounty-hunter friends" had taken an extremely gung ho approach, but they'd gotten the job done.

"I think the First Strike bounty hunters should be congratulated," she said, reversing her earlier opinion, now that she'd had time to consider it. "They saved my life. This Paulie Sapp character was over the edge, and I believe he *was* going to kill me." And she related the whole story to Palmer, tiptoeing around Gavin's radical rescue.

She did not want to give the police any excuse to file charges against Gavin.

She did not want him to return to prison.

The strength of her feelings surprised her, but they were undeniable.

Shelby finished up with Lyle as quickly as she could. Jake was being pretty good, since someone had rustled up some juice and a couple of cookies for him. But his angelic behavior would last only so long. Normally the police wouldn't have allowed a child to stay in the room with her during questioning, but she'd balked at being separated from him, and they'd relented. She was, after all, a victim, not a suspect.

Lyle's questions were, as she'd expected, superficial. He'd already known what he thought he needed to know before he entered the room; in his mind, his interview with Shelby was just a formality.

When he was done with her, she gratefully escaped the airless room. Then she remembered she had no car. She would have to call someone to pick her up.

She spotted a reporter from the local TV station lurking on the front steps of the police station and veered in a different direction. She wasn't up to media interviews. She was about to duck into the ladies' room to regroup when she spotted another familiar face—this one much more welcome. Rosie Amadeo was trotting up the steps toward the glass doors, her face etched with deep lines of worry.

She smiled, though, when she saw Shelby, then enveloped both her and Jake into a big hug and burst into tears. "I came as soon as I heard," she sobbed. "I can't believe this has happened to you *again!* I just feel so guilty!"

"Guilty?" Shelby disentangled herself from Rosie's tenacious hug.

"Paulie Sapp was *my* parolee. My God, I should have seen this coming. I should have recognized the signs that he was unraveling."

"Oh, Rosie, honey. You know as well as I do that you can't always tell when these guys are going haywire."

"But he was creepy. I should have watched him closer."

"I'm sure you did everything by the book. Now don't give it another thought."

Rosie wiped her tears away and laughed. "Look at me. I should be comforting you, not the other way around. Are you okay? Really? Oh, look at your poor face, all those scratches. And your nylons and—oh! Not your Prada shoes."

" 'Fraid so."

"Let's go home to my house. You probably haven't eaten, and you know my mom loves to feed you. Jake, too."

"Thanks for the offer, Rosie, but I really just want to go home. I need to shower and change clothes. Can you drive me?"

"Sure, kid. Here, let me take Jake."

Shelby gratefully turned her toddler over to Rosie, then hobbled down the steps, wishing she'd worn a coat today. Then she noticed a black Blazer with tinted windows parked at the curb. Black Blazers were common enough cars, but this one…

Sure enough, the driver's window slid down. Gavin was behind the wheel.

"Just a minute, Rosie." She limped over to the Blazer. For a few moments all she could do was just look at him, so big and sturdy. A bruise was forming on his left cheekbone, and he had a small cut on his chin. "I owe you an apology," she finally said. "And a big thank-you. What you did might have been a little crazy, but you risked your life for me."

"Then you're not going to revoke my—"

"Don't be ridiculous. Of course not." Was that the only reason he'd waited out here? To find out if he was going back to jail? After the way she'd treated him earlier, she wasn't surprised he would be worried about his future, but she'd hoped he was hanging out for some other reason.

To offer her a ride home, maybe.

"Well, I'll see you in a couple of weeks," she finished lamely.

He nodded. "I'm looking forward to it." The warmth in his voice made her insides go liquid, and she realized her feelings were wholly inappropriate, and way beyond the initial attraction she'd acknowledged this morning. It was the White Knight Syndrome, she told herself. She would just simply instruct herself to get over it. And she would.

In about a million years.

Chapter Three

Two weeks and three days had passed since Shelby's aborted kidnapping. Each day that week, Gavin had expected Shelby to walk through the door for the follow-up inspection she'd promised. And each hour she didn't show up made Gavin increasingly antsy.

The loft was ready. Six to eight hours a day working on it every evening, plus more on the weekends, had made an incredible difference. Most of the junk had been hauled away, the plank floor stripped and varnished, the grimy windows washed until they sparkled. Rex Bettencourt had come up with some used bathroom fixtures in almost mint condition for a ridiculously low price—Gavin didn't want to know from where. And he'd helped Gavin install them for free. He'd also brought the wiring up to code. They'd found the loft's original light fixtures, and now the whole space could be brightly illuminated at night.

Though he didn't have the resources to install a real kitchen, he built some doors for the existing cabinets along one wall. Rex found him an apartment-size refrigerator, and Lori gave him an extra microwave oven she'd inherited from a college roommate.

Furniture was scavenged from everywhere. What couldn't be refinished or repaired was painted over to disguise flaws. His sister, Aubrey, had brought over some pictures for the walls, things from his old house that she'd kept safe for him—mostly old prints that had belonged to their grandparents.

The end result surprised even Gavin. He'd never imagined the grungy loft could be transformed into such a cool living space.

Between his efforts in the loft and his job, he hadn't had much time to make over the First Strike office—and frankly, he got the idea that his fellow bounty hunters wouldn't be too grateful if he spiffed the place up too much. They had a certain image to maintain, after all. But he'd gotten rid of the dirty towels, old magazines, beer bottles and pizza boxes. He just hoped Shelby arrived soon. He wanted her official seal of approval so he could stop worrying about it.

He also wanted to talk to her about something else. The fact that Shelby had endured two kidnapping attempts in two days worried the hell out of him. She'd chalked it up to coincidence and bad luck, and he supposed that was possible. Her job demanded that she mix with a lot of nasty people, and it wasn't uncommon for parole officers to receive threats or suffer violence. But Gavin's cop instincts were still fully functional, and it didn't feel right to him.

So he'd done a little checking. And he'd turned up an interesting factoid.

"Watching out the window won't make her show up any quicker," Beau commented lazily. He'd been sitting across from Gavin at the reception desk, going over a case Beau wanted Gavin to work on.

"Ah, hell, I can't help it. I'm just nervous."

"What have you got to worry about? Your place looks great. Hell, it's nicer than the house you had before."

Gavin shook his head. "You don't know Shelby. She's so…fastidious. What if she checks to see whether I have hot water? The water heater Rex got me keeps blowing out the electricity, so I had to turn it off."

But Beau had zeroed in on one word. "Fastidious?"

"You know, real persnickety. Wears perfectly pressed silk suits and her nail polish is never chipped. And her shoes, oh, my God—"

A slow grin spread over Beau's face. "Oh, I got it. You have a thing for her."

"What? You gotta be kidding."

"You always did have a thing for the squeaky-clean good girls—the pretty cheerleaders, the teacher's pets, the choir girls."

"And you always went for the trashy sluts," Gavin countered, trying to focus attention away from himself.

"I went for the ones I thought I could get," Beau argued, chewing thoughtfully on the end of his pen. "You, on the other hand, only seemed to want a girl when she was out of your league—which this Shelby Dorsey—"

"Dorset. Shelby Dorset."

"Whatever. She's obviously not the type who would have anything to do with you. Which is exactly why she turns you on. Unhealthy pattern, my man." He lowered his voice. "What about Lori? She doesn't have a boyfriend. Why don't you ask her out?"

"Lori? That woman scares the hell out of me. She's got a black belt in karate or something."

"Tae kwon do," Beau corrected him.

"Whatever. She's pretty, I guess, in an outdoorsy way, but definitely not my style."

"And Shelby *is* your style?"

"No! I didn't say that."

Beau just grinned. Damn it, his best friend knew him way too well. "Didn't you say she was married anyway?"

"I thought she was at first. She's got a kid. But she's divorced." When he'd been looking for ties between Paulie Sapp and Manny Cruz, he'd also snooped a bit into Shelby's background to find out if she had any other connections to the two men. He'd turned up all sorts of intriguing bits about his parole officer, including the fact her father was a prominent state senator and a childhood friend of the governor.

"Probably hates men," Beau concluded. "Best not to even contemplate—"

"Jeez, Maddox, I'm not stupid enough to make a play for my parole officer." But that didn't stop him from fantasizing about it.

She turned up just before lunch. Her suit was shell-pink wool with a pale pink silk blouse. Pink leather pumps, three-inch heels. Gold locket at her neck. Tiny gold hoop earrings.

Gavin catalogued all of these things in an instant— a habit he'd developed as a cop, and another instinct that would probably be with him always.

Rex chose that moment to show up with lunch, two take-out pizzas from Mama Leone's down the block. At least Shelby would know he wasn't starving.

"Oh, hey, nice to meet you," Rex said when he was introduced. Using a paper napkin, he wiped pizza grease off his hand, then held it out to Shelby, who took it politely. "We've heard a lot about you."

"You look great," Lori added. "The scratches on your face are all gone."

Gavin winced, wishing Lori wouldn't bring up any reminders of that awful day.

"I'm a fast healer," Shelby said, sounding embarrassed. "But I did want to thank you and Ace again—and of course, Gavin. I was so distracted that day I'm afraid I didn't react very well. You all risked your lives for me, and if there's anything I can do—"

"Just take care of Gavin," Ace said. "Treat him right. He's already proved himself an asset to First Strike, and I want to hang on to him."

"I will do my best," she said, finally turning her attention to Gavin. "Can we…?" She nodded upward.

"Sure." He wondered why she couldn't bring herself to say, *Let's go up to your apartment.* Because it sounded risqué, maybe, though everyone here knew she had perfectly legitimate reasons for going upstairs with Gavin. And risqué was one word that did not describe Shelby Dorset.

SHELBY COULDN'T BELIEVE what her eyes told her. "Are you sure this is the same place?" she asked Gavin, dumbfounded as she took in the huge, airy loft. Sunlight from the crisp November day streamed in through the floor-to-ceiling windows, illuminating the immaculate, shiny wood floor. He'd put in a kitchen—well, sort of a kitchen—with an oak table and four high-backed chairs. There was actually a bowl of fruit on the table. A worn but comfy-looking sofa and two mismatched chairs and some scarred tables defined a living area in the center.

Then there was the bedroom area, partially separated by a Chinese folding screen. A metal clothes rack held a few shirts and a pair of khaki slacks on coat hangers. An antique dresser with a mirror was angled into a corner.

But the bed was what drew her attention. It was huge, and it had the most scrumptious-looking purple-and-white-striped comforter with matching pillows. The platform base was painted purple to match. It was like something out of a chichi bed-and-bath catalogue.

He even had pictures on the walls.

"My sister, Aubrey, helped decorate," he said, sounding embarrassed. He was probably humiliated to be a he-man with a clean, sharply decorated apartment. But Shelby thought it was wonderful. Lord, what fun to live in a place like this, where you could see the whole sky out the windows or watch the traffic and the people. To be right here in the middle of things, instead of in some boring subdivision where every house looked the same and the quiet could kill you.

She inspected the bathroom, which was brightly lit, with modern, clean fixtures expertly installed—and plush, dark purple towels. There was even a silver-framed Mexican mirror over the sink.

"You have really created a miracle," she finally said. "But I have to ask the obvious. How did you pay for it all?"

"I knocked off a liquor store."

She bristled. "It was an honest question and deserves an honest answer."

"Sorry. I've spent most of my life having people be suspicious of me. Sometimes it was deserved, but most of the time it wasn't. I didn't have to pay for any of this stuff, except with my own sweat. Rex found the bathroom fixtures—I didn't ask him where. He's a former marine whose main skill is acquisition. The other guys and Lori and my sister scrounged through their attics and garages and came up with all the rest. I did buy the mattress, sheets and towels new. I've had enough of lumpy, industrial-grade prison mattresses and dingy, threadbare sheets and towels to last a lifetime."

Now she felt crummy for even asking. Clean, crisp sheets, big, fluffy towels—these were things she took for granted. She needed a reminder now and then that even simple pleasures weren't an automatic privilege.

She made a quick doodle in her notebook to hide her discomfort. Then she walked back to the kitchen-dining area and pulled out a chair. "Let me go through the list of questions real fast, and you'll be rid of me until next month."

He sighed. "Okay. Here, I'll save you the trouble. No, I haven't used any illegal drugs. No, I haven't associated with anyone using illegal drugs. No, I haven't touched any firearms. Yes, I associated with people who use firearms. They're all licensed to carry. No, I haven't associated with any persons engaged in criminal activities other than the subjects of my skip tracing, and then only over the phone or computer. Yes, I have actively associated with one ex-convict, Ace, whom we've discussed before. I have $228 in the bank and all debts paid, and…I'm not having any problems. Did that cover it?"

Shelby wrote quickly, scanning her standard checklist. She knew this was humiliating for Gavin and she sought to get through the rest of the interview as quickly as possible. "I think that covers it. Let's meet again on December 12 at…nine in the morning?"

"That's fine."

She closed her notebook. "You can always call me if you have any problems."

"That's it? I don't have to pee in a cup?"

"Not today. You obviously haven't had time to do drugs if you were doing all this." She gestured toward the loft.

Finally he smiled. But he quickly sobered. "There is something else I wanted to discuss with you. But it's about your problem, not mine."

"My problem?"

"Your recent attractiveness to kidnappers. Something didn't sit right with me about what happened to you. So I looked into it."

"You…what?"

"My job involves tracking people down, checking up on them. While I was at it, I checked up on Manny Cruz and Paulie Sapp. Sapp said he was one of your parolees, but he wasn't."

Shelby wasn't sure how she felt about one of her cases investigating *her*. It was supposed to be the other way around. The fact that Gavin Schuyler had so much information at his fingertips was slightly unsettling. He could probably find out anything about her—her phone number, her address, what size bra she wore. He'd been a cop, a detective.

She sat up a little straighter. "I'm aware Sapp wasn't one of my cases," she said. "I checked my own files. I didn't think he looked familiar."

"So the story he told about wanting revenge against

you 'cause you were some kind of ball breaker—that was bull."

"I know. Which throws his whole story into question. Detective Palmer thinks he made up the stuff about holding me for ransom so he wouldn't have to admit he was going to kill me." She said this as dispassionately as she could. But Lyle's follow-up phone call, received the previous week, had unnerved her terribly.

Owen had been right in some respects. Her job did put her at risk. Sapp had probably spotted her when he'd come into the office for his visits with Rosie. Then again, if he'd wanted to rape and murder, he could have picked any woman off the street. Why her?

"Also, Sapp didn't have a history of kidnapping or murder. Domestic abuse, yeah. Armed robbery. But not kidnapping."

"I know that, too. It's possible he's done it and never been caught." Although privately, she thought he was too stupid to not get caught. "Or he could have been escalating. Murderers usually don't start with killing. They work up to it." But of course he knew that.

"And did you also know that your ex-husband once defended Sapp on a drug charge? It was several years ago, when Sapp first moved to this area—before the armed robbery that got him put away."

Perspiration broke out on the back of Shelby's neck and along her hairline, though it wasn't warm up here. "No, I didn't know that."

"It might be a coincidence. Owen Dorset has defended literally hundreds of criminals, no doubt many of whom have entered the probation system. Still, I think you should be careful. And don't take for granted any of the wild guesses Lyle Palmer hands you as definitive conclusions. The guy's a putz."

He paused a beat, looking into her eyes. She caught her breath at the power of his full attention.

"Would your husband have any reason to want to do away with you?" he asked slowly.

This was getting ridiculous. "Of course not. He would much rather keep me alive so he can torture me. Gavin, I appreciate your concern. And I know it's your natural inclination to want to investigate a crime. But, really, you should leave this to the cops."

She knew she'd made a mistake the second the words left her mouth. Gavin had been a cop—one of the best, from what she'd heard.

He got a stony look on his face. "I don't want to see anything happen to you."

"I know." She reached out and squeezed his arm, then wished she hadn't. She wasn't supposed to have any physical contact with her male cases, other than a handshake. The move had been an impulsive one, because she really was touched that he would care enough to check things out for her on his own time. "I'll be fine. And I guarantee, I'll never get into a car again without checking the back seat first."

She rose, intending to get out of there. She couldn't quite get that beautiful bed, looking like a plum-swirl sundae, out of her head.

"Do you carry a gun?" Gavin asked as he walked her to the door.

"Heavens, no."

"Would you like to? One of the guys could probably get you one and train you to—"

"No. I don't like guns and I have a young child. I don't want a gun anywhere near him." Owen would have a fit, probably use it as an excuse to wrest custody of Jake away from her. That was what he'd wanted when they first separated. Full custody of Jake—with her paying child support based on the income she received from a trust, which far outstripped her salary. Thank God, the judge had been sensible.

"Do you have any self-defense training?" he asked as he locked the door behind them.

"Not really. I took a class at the Y once."

He paused before they entered the back door of First Strike, his breath steaming in the cold. "Lori has a black belt in tae kwon do. She would love to teach you some self-defense techniques. Even if you're right, and the kidnapping attempts were a coincidence—you never know when you might need to fend someone off."

Shelby knew she should politely but firmly turn down Gavin's attempts to be of service. He already knew too much about her. He knew about her ex-husband and her son. Probably knew a lot more he wasn't telling her.

But she was undeniably intrigued by the idea of learning nonlethal self-defense from Lori Bettencourt, who was herself a fascinating character. Shelby thought of Lori as a Charlie's Angel candidate—tough, capable, but very human. And as different from Shelby as an alley cat to a pampered Persian.

And it would give you another link to Gavin, an intrusive little voice reminded her. It was the voice of her conscience, which never let her get away with anything. Darn it.

"I'll talk to her," Shelby said noncommittally.

"GAVIN, COME HERE. I need a man."

Now those were words guaranteed to pique Gavin's interest. He looked up from his desk where he'd been doing Internet searches on Manny Cruz. He had continued investigating the two men who had assaulted Shelby, determined to find a link between them. But he only did it on his own time. Ace had made it clear that Gavin's time should be spent on cases that would pay the bills.

In truth, this particular search could have waited until tomorrow morning. But it had been damn difficult to leave the office when Shelby was here in gym shorts and a snug T-shirt, getting self-defense instruction from Lori.

Apparently he wasn't the only one intrigued by the possibility of watching two attractive women grapple with each other. Beau, Rex and Ace had all found excuses to work late. The place was like Grand Central Station.

Lori was the one who'd called to Gavin.

"You got a roomful of men here," he answered her.

"I need someone big and tall to attack me."

"Gee, that's an attractive invitation. But I'm fond of most of my internal organs and I don't want them spread all over the floor."

"Come on, Gavin," Shelby said. "I really need some help here. I'm completely hopeless. Anyway, this whole thing was your idea."

Gavin would never have hung around if he'd known this was going to be a participatory sport. He was much more comfortable watching Shelby from the corner of his eye, and he certainly didn't want to touch her.

Still, to refuse might seem churlish. With a sense of

foreboding, he stood and joined the women in the center of the room, where Lori had laid down some mats.

Shelby looked a lot different today. Without the power suit and the heels, she seemed softer, more human. Her shoulder-length hair was in a loose ponytail, giving her a youthful appearance. But it was her face that he really noticed. When doing her job, she wore an impersonal, professional mask. But with Lori, she was a student. Her expression was open, curious, friendly.

He didn't really want to be this close to her, where her scent hung in the air from her mild exertion. Hell, he could see the outline of her bra through the thin T-shirt. One of her straps was twisted. The imperfection was endearing. Now those were two words he'd never have thought would apply to Shelby Dorset.

"What do you want me to do?" he asked Lori.

"Pretend you're a mugger. Come up behind me and grab me." She turned around and stood obligingly still.

"Okeydokey." He placed a hand on each of her shoulders.

"Something a little more convincing, please. You're a mugger, not my dance partner."

With a sigh he slung his right arm around her neck and put her in a choke hold. Then he grabbed her left wrist.

"Good," Lori said as Shelby studied them intently. "There are a couple of ways to get out of this one. Start by backing up and leaning into his chest. That loosens his hold a bit. Tuck your chin so he can't choke you." She demonstrated, and Gavin took a step backward to balance himself.

"You've got one free hand," Lori continued, wiggling the fingers of her right hand. "Lots of things you can do with it. You can reach back and pull his hair." She demonstrated, though she didn't pull hard. "You can scratch the face, poke at the eyes. You can use the elbow to the ribs."

Thankfully she didn't actually carry out any of these techniques, though she came too close for comfort.

"But here's my technique of choice. It's especially good for women who wear high heels. Take out the knee with your heel."

Gavin did his best to avoid Lori's kick. But instead of kicking him, she hooked her foot around the back of his knee and tugged, throwing him off balance again.

"Then you roll him over your hip and onto the floor. Stomp on his face to make sure he stays where you put him."

Gavin found himself flat on his back, Lori's bare foot an inch from his nose. He wasn't even sure how he'd gotten here. He'd learned some basic martial-arts moves at the police academy, but Lori was in a whole other league.

Shelby's china-blue eyes were alight with interest. "I want to learn how to do that!"

"So do I," Gavin murmured.

"I can show you," Lori said, obviously pleased that she was finally getting a little respect around here. "Shelby, you stand here. Gavin, just grab her like you did me."

"No, no, no. Ms. Dorset is my parole officer. I can't—"

"Oh, come on, Gavin," Shelby said impatiently. "I'm not in parole-officer mode right now, so it's okay."

She definitely wasn't, but that didn't make it okay.

"C'mon, Schuyler," Beau goaded him. "Don't be a wuss."

When he was sure the women couldn't see, he shot Beau a rude gesture. Then he gamely put his arm around Shelby's neck and grabbed her wrist as firmly as he dared.

Oh, God, she felt really different from Lori. She was so much softer, so much more…womanly. No other word for it. And his body responded in a typically masculine fashion. *Think cold water. Icy shower. Being buried in a glacier.* He was just starting to retrieve control when Shelby, under Lori's tutelage, started pummeling him—all the same moves Lori had used, but without Lori's control. Her fingers actually made contact with his eye and the elbow in the ribs would leave a bruise.

"Now the knee," Lori instructed.

No matter how much he didn't want to injure his parole officer, he wasn't taking a kick in the knee—his bad leg, too. He was tired of being the passive punching bag. He pulled a maneuver of his own—mostly instinctual—by dropping and rolling, taking Shelby with him. In a split second he had her on her face on the mat, her arm bent behind her, his other hands reaching for the cuffs that he no longer carried on his belt.

The minute he realized what he'd done, he released her. "Damn it. Sorry, Ms. Dorset. I didn't hurt you, did I?"

She rolled over and gazed up at him, a strange expression on her face. "No. But that was a nice move." She took his proffered hand and allowed him to pull her to her feet.

"Wanta try that move on me, tough guy?" Lori challenged. She turned to Shelby. "Power helps, but with most of this, it's balance rather than strength. And we women are lower to the ground and have better balance than these male giants."

He didn't want to try anything on Lori. He had a feeling the woman could hurt him if she wanted to. But Lori insisted she needed to show Shelby how to defend against his move. So he cooperated. Gradually some of his old self-defense training came back, and Lori didn't dispatch him as easily as she thought she would. But eventually he ended up on the mat again.

"If you can grab his pinkie finger," Lori said, "you can control him with almost no effort."

"Let me try," Shelby said eagerly. "That looks like one I can do."

"Aw, come on, have pity," Gavin complained. "Beau, you get up here and let the ladies beat you up."

Beau shook his head. "Aubrey would ask too many questions about the bruises."

"Rex?"

"Not Rex," Lori objected. "His marine commando tricks outstrip my skills any day. Ace?"

"Thought you'd never ask." He grinned, only it was more of a leer. There was sort of an odd chemistry between Lori and Ace. He was her father's best friend, the shoulder she'd cried on when Glenn had been murdered, her mentor and her boss. But they fought like siblings and they conspired like best friends. Beau had assured him there was nothing romantic between them, and in all honesty, Gavin hadn't seen any real evidence of that. Still, sometimes he just got this feeling....

Gavin's male ego was slightly soothed when Ace, Vietnam vet and ex-con, ended up on the mat at least as many times as Gavin had. Lori was kind of scary—in a totally cute way.

Then Ace retired from the action, claiming a bad back. As the women finished up their lesson, Gavin pulled up a chair next to Ace. "I found out something about this Manny Cruz that might or might not matter," he said.

"Manny who?"

"The guy who offed himself in Shelby's office."

"Oh."

"A few months ago he was working at a lube shop. It's around the corner from where Owen Dorset lives."

"Owen who?"

Ace's attention was still focused on the women. Gavin resisted the urge to knock him up the side of the head. "Shelby's ex. At lunch I stopped in and got a guy to check their records. Owen takes his car there."

Now Ace was tracking. "So there's a possible connection between Owen and one of the kidnappers."

"*Both* of the kidnappers. He once defended Paulie Sapp on a drug charge. Of course, Owen Dorset has defended half the criminal population of Payton at one time or another."

"Still, it's interesting. Have you told Shelby?"

"Not yet. I don't want her running to Owen with accusations. If I'm wrong, it'll just piss him off. And if I'm right, it could put Shelby in danger."

"Or you. Listen, Schuyler, I don't want to put a damper on things, and I know you feel like since you saved the woman's life you're sort of stuck protecting her. But this is not a case that will pay the bills around here. You really need to focus on investigations that promise a paycheck."

"I'm doing it on my own time," Gavin said, bristling slightly, though he supposed that, given the crime he'd been convicted of, Ace had a perfect right to be suspicious of what Gavin might be doing while on the First Strike time clock.

"Oh, hell, son, I'm not criticizing. You've been doing a bang-up job so far. It's just easy to get obsessed with something. And when it comes to a woman like her, it's hard not to get obsessed. If you know what I mean."

Gavin was afraid he did. He took the warning to heart. He'd thought he was doing a good job hiding the lust he felt for Shelby Dorset, but Ace had apparently seen the truth. Did Shelby know, too?

"Don't tell her anything yet," Ace said. "Maybe you should talk to this Sapp guy."

Chapter Four

Shelby's body felt pleasantly stretched after her first self-defense lesson. She was probably going to have a couple of bruises, too. But she'd enjoyed the workout, enjoyed discovering she didn't have to be a helpless victim if a man with superior strength attacked her.

She'd changed out of her workout clothes in the First Strike office bathroom, feeling a little odd standing in her bra and panties, knowing one of her parolees was in the outer office only a few feet away.

It was odd enough he'd seen her in shorts and a T-shirt, weirder still that he'd had physical contact with her. There'd been nothing improper about it, of course. She'd insisted he help with the lesson, after all, and she was the one who'd stated they weren't in their usual roles.

Still, when she'd found herself facedown on the mat with Gavin on top of her, it had felt wholly improper. Or maybe it was just that her reaction to him was less than professional. She stared at herself in the mirror as she relived those few moments, saw the change in her face and wondered if anyone else had noticed.

Shaking herself, she ran a comb through her hair,

pinned it up in a quick twist, then emerged to find the office deserted except for Lori.

"Where'd everybody go?"

"You expected them to stay after the show was over? They're guys, after all. Jeez, the looks on their faces. You'd think we were mud wrestling or something."

"You mean they were here just to watch us?"

"The guys are never in the office after five o'clock. Next time, I say we charge admission. Hey, you want to go get something to eat? I mean, you probably need to get home or something…"

Shelby was surprised to hear a woman so confident with her physical self sounding suddenly so uncertain.

"Sure, I'm starving. Where do you want to go?"

"Dudley's Blue Note has fettucini Alfredo to die for."

"Let's do it, then. My treat, since you won't let me pay you for the lessons."

"Hey, the lessons are fun for me, too. When else do I get the chance to throw my boss on the ground and stomp his face?"

They took Lori's ancient gray van, which she called "the Peepmobile." With its mirrored bubble windows on each side, it was the perfect surveillance vehicle.

It was only a few blocks to Dudley's Blue Note, an old-style bar that had become a favorite hangout for cops and lawyers. Shelby had been there a few times, though she'd discovered it wasn't a place to come alone unless you wanted to get hit on.

They took a booth in the back.

"So are you and Ace dating?" Shelby asked.

"Me and Ace?" Lori hooted with laughter. "Where

did you get a crazy idea like that? He's old enough to be my father."

"Nothing wrong with a May-December romance."

"Listen, I might be hard up, but dating Ace would be positively Freudian. He's known me since I was a baby. He used to dandle me on his knee. Did someone tell you we were sleeping together?" she asked, sounding appalled.

"No, no. I just thought I saw a spark or something. The way you two banter. Just a guess. Wrong, as it turns out. Forget I said anything. And what do you mean, hard up? You're bound to have guys lining up. You're smart, pretty, athletic and you have a cool job."

"Yeah, the cool job *is* the problem. Most guys do not like women who can beat them up."

"That's a very sexist attitude."

"Unfortunately, the male ego is a fragile thing, and it doesn't take much to crush it. The first time I change my own tire or beat a guy at one-on-one basketball, he's history."

"That's not a problem I've ever encountered," Shelby said.

"Yeah, you're pretty much a girlie-girl. Though you do have a macho job."

"Not really. It's more like baby-sitting than anything."

"Except the babies carry knives and guns."

They talked about innocuous things until their food arrived. Then Lori got a very intense look on her face. "Listen, there's something I want to ask you. You know who my father was, right?"

"Glenn Bettencourt. I knew him by reputation only, but he was something of a legend." *Hang 'em High Bettencourt.* That had been his nickname, but Shelby didn't think it was prudent to bring that up. "It was terrible, what happened to him."

"The police did a completely pathetic job investigating," Lori said. "They claimed it had to be one of the criminals he'd sentenced—and there'd been hundreds over his career. They found virtually no physical evidence, no witnesses, no clues of any kind. The case went cold almost immediately. Not long ago they released some of his personal effects to me, including his wallet. I was taking the photos out of the wallet when this little key fell out." She pulled a tiny gold key out of her purse and handed it to Shelby.

"Do you know what it goes to?"

"I didn't at first. But it looked familiar, and finally it hit me. It was *my* key. It goes to a jewelry box I got when I was about seven. You know, with a little ballerina that spins around?"

Shelby nodded. "I have one, too."

"One of my mother's continual efforts to interest me in girlie things. Anyway, I never used it. I stuck it in the top of my closet and forgot about it. So what would my father be doing with the key?"

Shelby leaned forward, her plate of pasta forgotten. Lori was spinning a good story. "So, don't leave me in suspense. You got the key, opened the jewelry box, and a threatening letter fell out."

"Almost. I found this. It's a little ledger book for a company called Canel Engineering. But there's no such company. I've searched every source I could think of."

Shelby examined the tiny, leather-bound black book. "CANEL ENG" was written on the first page; then the pages were filled with names—E. G. Capshaw. P. F.

Garland—along with amounts of money. The amounts were substantial, none under ten thousand dollars and many of them much more.

"Your father's handwriting?" Shelby asked.

Lori nodded uncomfortably. "Any way you look at it, it's bad. Maybe dad was loan sharking. Or keeping an alternate set of books for some company that's cheating the IRS."

"You should probably turn this over to the cops," Shelby said reluctantly.

"I made copies and sent them to Detective Palmer. I don't think Lyle ever did anything with them."

Shelby groaned. "That turkey. Who is he sleeping with to get all these high-profile cases assigned to him?"

Lori laughed. "So you've got Lyle figured out."

"Would you mind if I kept this book for a few days?" Shelby asked. "I can search for these names in our database. If any of these guys are bad dudes your dad put away, chances are they've passed through our office." It was a long shot. But if Lyle was just going to sit on the information, what harm would it do for Shelby to at least check?

"Sure, keep it. I made an extra copy."

"Wanta go grab some lunch?" Beau asked Gavin the following afternoon. "You've had your nose to the grindstone all morning."

Gavin looked up from the arrest record he was studying. For a moment his eyes refused to focus. Then Beau's face became clear. "I have some personal errands to run during lunch."

"You gotta eat. C'mon, Schuyler. We don't punch a

clock around here. Ace isn't going to fire you if you take a few extra minutes for lunch. Especially not with the results you're producing."

Gavin stretched. "I know. I'm just so grateful to have a decent job, I don't want to blow it."

"You won't." Beau grabbed the folder and slapped it closed. "Let's go get some barbecue. Man, you've really changed. I remember those three-hour lunches at Dudley's when you were in uniform."

"I was cultivating informants," Gavin said with a grin as he grabbed his scruffy leather jacket from the back of his chair. But he grew serious again. "I have changed, Beau. Prison ruins some men, but it made me better. I did what I had to to get out as fast as I could, and I'll do what I have to so that I never have to go back. Ever."

Beau's face was grim as they climbed into his black Mustang. "Was it really bad?" he asked. "Bad, like what you read about and see in the movies?" They'd never talked about this before, and Gavin knew Beau still felt guilty for his part in sending Gavin up the river.

"You mean, was I girlfriend to some guy named Bubba with no neck? No, it wasn't that bad. I got beat up a few times. But that wasn't the worst of it. The bad food, the hard bed, the subhuman roommate, going stir crazy, none of that was as bad as the fact that I just…couldn't leave."

"Uh, wouldn't be much of a prison if—"

"I'm not going back. No way, for no one. I'll never take simple freedoms for granted again. None of us should."

"Hell, after almost getting blown up last summer, I don't take *anything* for granted anymore."

Gavin laughed suddenly. "Well, this is a cheery conversation."

"Yeah, let's change the subject. What errands do you have to run?"

"I'm going to pay a visit to Paulie Sapp. He already made bail, can you believe it?"

"'Course I can. He was probably out before the police finished questioning you. Listen, Gav, you really ought to let this one go. The cops will handle it."

"Palmer? Huh. He'll handle it like he handles everything—it'll go right down the toilet." And he told Beau what he'd learned about Cruz and Sapp, that they both had a connection to Owen Dorset. He could see that Beau was intrigued.

"I can see why you'd want to follow up," Beau conceded. "Just don't let it get out of hand. No paycheck at the end of that case."

"Yeah, yeah, Ace already warned me."

"Want me to go with you to see Sapp?"

"Nah, I can handle him."

AN HOUR LATER, Gavin deeply regretted turning down Beau's offer of company.

Paulie Sapp lived in the corner unit of a decaying apartment building not far from the First Strike offices, so Gavin was able to walk there, which was a good thing. His heap of a car was out of commission until he installed a new water pump.

As he approached the building, Gavin noted Sapp's car, a pockmarked Pinto, sitting in front of his building. A TV was blaring from the upstairs window. Sounded like his man was home.

Gavin reached reflexively for his sidearm, then realized for the umpteenth time he didn't carry one anymore. He felt naked without a weapon. Sapp wasn't likely to welcome Gavin with open arms, and the only protection Gavin had on him was pepper spray. Well, no use delaying. He walked up the creaking stairs and banged on Sapp's door. Nothing.

He banged harder and the door fell open. Apparently it hadn't been latched. "Sapp?" he called out. "Hey, Paulie Sapp, you home?"

Nothing except a slight odor wafting out the door that made Gavin's nose twitch. Oh, no. Surely not. He nudged the door farther open, but it caught on something and stopped. A foot.

"Paulie, you stupid SOB," Gavin muttered. He stuck his head inside the door. Paulie Sapp lay dead on the floor, his chest blown open by a large-caliber gun. From the look of him, he hadn't been dead long. His TV played to an empty living room. A six-pack of beer sat on the coffee table, one can pulled free of the others, sitting open. The can still had sweat on it.

Sweating a bit himself, Gavin backed out of the apartment. Again he reached for his belt, this time looking for a radio that wasn't there. He cursed, then walked across the hall and banged on Paulie's neighbor's door. He could hear a TV behind this door, too. After an interminable amount of time, the door opened a crack and a rheumy eye peeked out, deeply suspicious.

"Excuse me, ma'am, but I need to use your phone. There's been an accident across the hall."

SHELBY'S PHONE CHIRPED as she was leaving the office parking lot. She frowned and pulled over, then dug through her purse to find the thing. She'd gotten the phone mainly for emergencies. Only Owen, the day-care center and her supervisor had the number. So it always made her stomach churn when it rang.

She flipped it open. "Hello?"

"Shelby, thank goodness." It was Rosie, who also had her number, Shelby remembered, though she'd never used it before.

"Are you okay?" Shelby asked.

"Yeah, I'm fine, but you'll never believe this. Paulie Sapp is dead. Someone shot him."

"Oh, my God."

"And that's not the worst of it. Your pretty boy is the prime suspect."

All the air whooshed out of Shelby's lungs. "My—Owen?"

"No, not Owen," Rosie said impatiently. "Gavin. He was the one who found the body, or so he says. He called it in from the neighbor's."

"Gavin Schuyler didn't shoot anyone," Shelby declared. "That's ridiculous." But this didn't look good. If Gavin was anywhere near Paulie Sapp, it had something to do with her. She was sure of that. "And someone should have notified me right away. I'm his parole officer."

"They tried. You'd already left for the day. I told Ramona I'd get hold of you."

That figured. The one day she'd actually left at 5:00, someone had called her at 5:01. "I'm going down to the station and see if I can straighten this out. Of course they would suspect Gavin first thing. He found the body, and he's a known felon. But there's no way he did it."

"You sound pretty sure of that. A few weeks ago, you

thought Gavin Schuyler was scum of the earth. 'A cop gone bad, nothing worse in my book,' I think were your words."

"I've gotten to know him better since then. He's really trying to turn his life around, Rosie. You should see what he did to this loft he moved into. The place was just a dump, and he made it beautiful." She hooked her seldom-used headset to the cell phone so she could drive, then pulled out into traffic. "I bought him a housewarming present," she confessed. It wasn't really proper for her to do such a thing. But she was so proud of the hard work he'd put in on his apartment, she'd wanted to positively enforce his behavior.

That was what she told herself, anyway.

"You're not going soft on me, are you?" Rosie asked. "I warned you when you first started working for the department that you couldn't afford to form any attachments to these guys. Almost all of them go back to jail no matter how hard you work to keep them clean, and it'll break your heart if you let it."

"Gavin's not going back to prison," Shelby said. "Listen, Rosie, thanks for passing the word along. I need to make a phone call."

"Okay. Call me at home later and let me know how everything goes."

Shelby hung up, then quickly dialed the number at First Strike. Maybe Gavin would answer the phone. Maybe the story of Gavin's arrest was bogus, or an exaggeration. But she got the answering machine. "Lori, I won't be able to make our self-defense lesson," she said into the machine. "I guess you probably know why."

WHEN SHE GOT TO THE STATION, a news van was already parked out front. With the story of her kidnapping still fresh on the reporters' minds, she didn't figure she could sneak into the building without being noticed, and she certainly didn't want to see her face on the news anymore. She idled at the curb, trying to figure out how to get in without being seen, when someone knocked on her window. She jumped so violently she almost hit her head on the roof of her car.

It was Lori, thank God. Shelby lowered the window.

"I thought I recognized your car," Lori said.

"Is it true? Did they arrest Gavin?" Shelby asked.

"What I heard is that he's being *detained* for questioning."

That wasn't the quite same as being arrested. Shelby took this as encouraging news. "But the rest is true? Paulie Sapp was murdered and Gavin found the body?"

Lori nodded. "Beau and Ace are already here with some lawyer. The good news is, Craig Cartwright's been assigned the case. He's Beau's old partner from when he was on the force, and he's a really good detective, really smart. He won't try to railroad Gavin."

"Then I guess I'm not needed," Shelby said, trying not to sound too forlorn. "Sounds like things are under control." She wasn't sure what she'd been thinking, rushing to the rescue like some avenging goddess. Plenty of the men and women she supervised got arrested. And while she was always sad and disappointed when they reoffended, and she felt that she'd failed them somehow, she never considered it an emergency when it happened.

"It probably wouldn't hurt to have you put in a good

word for him," Lori ventured. "I mean, if Craig's on the fence about arresting him…"

"All they have to do is run a gunshot residue test on his hand," Shelby said impatiently. "If it comes up positive, yeah, throw him behind bars. But if it's negative, that should satisfy everyone, right?"

Lori was looking at her with a sort of pitying expression on her face. "You've got the hots for him, don't you? It's understandable. He's got that Patrick-Swayze-bad-boy thing going. Makes him pretty dishy."

"I do *not* have the hots for him. I'm concerned. If one of my guys goes out and shoots someone, it's not a very good reflection on me, now, is it?"

"Whatever. Do you want to go inside with me and find out what's going on, or sit out here and worry?"

"I'll never get past the reporters."

Lori laughed. "Oh, so that's it. Come with me. I am the mistress of disguises."

Shelby was just desperate enough to do it. Yeah, okay, she had a little thing for Gavin. What red-blooded woman wouldn't? Rosie was always salivating over her parolees. She liked big men with tattoos, she said. And no one blinked, not even their superstern supervisor, Ramona. As long as Shelby's behavior was beyond reproach, she reasoned, she had nothing to feel guilty about. She couldn't help her lustful thoughts.

They walked to the Peepmobile and Lori opened the back doors. Inside, the vehicle had built-in compartments of all shapes and sizes stuffed with an odd array of camera equipment and other hardware as well as clothing, wigs and other odds and ends.

She hopped into the van and gave Shelby a hand up,

then shut the doors. "It won't take much to fool the re-porters. Let's see—put these on." She tossed a pair of painter's pants and a sweatshirt to Shelby. Five minutes later, wearing the baggy clothes, a short, red wig, glasses and dangly earrings, Shelby looked nothing like herself.

"Are you sure about this? If they catch me, it'll be really embarrassing."

"You'll be fine. I do good work. Last summer I tricked out Beau's wife like a biker chick—all leather and fake tattoos."

"Aubrey? Gavin's sister?" She'd met Aubrey Schuyler, now Aubrey Maddox, at Gavin's parole hear-ing. "She's a chemistry professor."

"When I was done with her, she looked distinctly *un*-professorial. Let's roll."

Lori was right. They strolled right past the reporters, who ignored them completely. Shelby approached the desk sergeant, a stern-looking woman whose leathery face advertised her as a lifetime pack-a-day smoker. "I'm looking for Gavin Schuyler. I understand he was brought in—"

"No reporters beyond those doors," the desk sergeant cut her off.

"I'm not a reporter. I'm his parole officer." Shelby flashed her ID.

"Oh. Why the bad disguise?"

"She's incognito," Lori said. "And it's *not* a bad disguise."

"Oh, you're the one from the newspaper," the desk sergeant said, suddenly all smiles. "Let me see what I can find out for you." But just then the double doors opened and Gavin appeared, flanked by Beau and Ace.

Shelby was so relieved to see him, she had to resist the inappropriate urge to run up and throw her arms around him. The men didn't notice her, so she stepped into their path. "They didn't arrest you?"

All three men stopped and stared at her. Gavin was the first to realize who she was. "Ms. Dorset?"

"Shh." She glanced over her shoulder to make sure no reporters were listening in. "It was Lori's idea."

But Beau and Ace weren't being quiet at all. They'd started laughing uncontrollably once they realized it was Shelby under the red wig and glasses.

"You guys knock it off," Lori scolded. "We're trying to avoid reporters here!"

But it was too late. A glossy brunette in heavy makeup, drawn by the commotion, approached them, motioning frantically for her cameraman to follow. "Excuse me. Gavin Schuyler? Did you kill Paulie Sapp? Was it some kind of revenge killing because of what he did to your parole officer?" She thrust the mike toward Gavin even as her feline eyes scanned the others, looking for familiar faces.

Her gaze fixed on Shelby. "Wait a minute. You're Shelby Dorset. What are you doing in that disguise?"

"What disguise?" Shelby said.

"WHAT DISGUISE?" Rosie repeated, then resumed her gales of laughter. "You couldn't come up with anything better?"

"I was under pressure," Shelby said. She took another bite of manicotti, courtesy of Rosie's mom, Nanette, who lived to cook for other people. "This is wonderful, Mrs. Amadeo. You should open a restaurant."

The tiny woman, who had the smooth, olive skin of someone much younger, beamed.

"Wait a minute," Rosie said. "You haven't finished the story."

"That was it," Shelby said. "Both Gavin and I declined to be interviewed, and the reporter actually respected our wishes."

"She must be new," Rosie said. "She still has a conscience."

"So this ex-convict," Nanette said suddenly. Shelby hadn't thought Rosie's mom had even been listening to the conversation. "He might still make a pretty good husband. He has a job, no?"

"Mama!" Rosie objected. "Please, stop looking for husbands for me under every rock. After my experience with the last one, I'm not anxious to repeat marriage."

"A woman's natural state is to be married," Nanette said. "You're still young, you can have lots of babies."

Rosie got a pained expression, and Shelby wanted to fold her friend into her arms. She knew Nanette meant well, but she wished Rosie's mom would give it a rest.

"Anyway," Nanette continued, "I wasn't talking about a husband for you. I mean for Shelby. Her face lights up when she talks about this Garth."

"Gavin," Rosie said, her ready smile returning. "What do you think, Shelby? Husband material?"

"I'm sure he'll make some woman a wonderful husband," Shelby said primly. "But I'm not exactly in the market for a new one, either. It's nice with just Jake and me." And she meant that. Between her job and her son, she had no time for meeting, dating, playing the stupid games you have to play to develop a relationship that might lead to marriage.

"You must bring your baby to visit," Nanette said. "I haven't seen him in months. When Rosie moves out, I will have an extra bedroom. Little Jake can come stay with me anytime."

Shelby stared at Rosie. "You're moving?"

"Oh, my gosh, I forgot to tell you. I finally found a nice apartment that I can actually afford. It's over near Skylark Meadows. It has trees all around and two swimming pools. I'm moving Saturday."

"That's so quick!" Shelby knew Rosie's stay with her mother was only supposed to be temporary, until she got back on her feet after the divorce. But the two of them seemed to get along so well. She mentioned this to Rosie later, when they went outside so Rosie could smoke. They sat on the porch swing, Shelby sipping on her second glass of rosé.

"I love my mother, you know that. But it's hard to date when you still live at home. She gives me a curfew, I swear."

Shelby giggled.

"I can't bring a guy over here, or she gives them the third degree. Asks them how much money they make. And that's one of the least intrusive questions. So this will be much better. I can still come visit—"

"And eat your mom's manicotti," Shelby added. "So, is there any man in particular? You haven't mentioned anyone lately." Which was a bit odd, because Rosie always had her eye on someone, at least theoretically.

She shrugged. "Nah. Haven't met anyone interesting.

But there are supposed to be lots of young singles at this complex. Hey, you can come hang out at my pool. Maybe we can *both* find guys. Unless, of course, you don't need to look anymore."

Shelby arched an eyebrow. "What's that supposed to mean?"

"Shelby and Gavin, sittin' in a tree, K-I-S-S—"

"Oh, stop it!" Shelby yelled, embarrassed. But also heated at the very thought of kissing Gavin Schuyler.

Chapter Five

"You'll just have to take him," Owen said. "This is a re-ally important meeting." He plopped Jake down on Shelby's living-room rug as if he were a sack of potatoes.

"Owen, I can't! I have plans!"

Owen, tall and lean and too handsome for his own good, arched one well-shaped brow at Shelby. "Don't tell me you have a date."

Like that would be impossible? But she wasn't going to get in a stupid argument about her social life with her ex-husband. "My plans are none of your concern, except to know that I have them and they can't be changed." In truth, she could cancel. She was supposed to meet Lori at the First Strike office for another self-defense lesson, her third. It wouldn't be a big deal to call Lori and reschedule. But she'd been looking forward to the lesson all day. She really liked Lori, she enjoyed the physical activity. Lord knew, she needed to get more exercise, and she didn't need to spend any more evenings at home, moping.

"You're always saying you don't get to spend enough time with Jake. Well, I'm giving you a bonus evening with him. Now, you don't want to see him?"

Jake looked up at Shelby with his big, blue eyes. He knew they were talking about him, and he sensed the tension. He didn't miss much.

Shelby walked over and picked up her son, cuddling him. "Of course I want to spend time with him. But I can't just drop everything at a moment's notice. If you'd called and asked me I could have rearranged my schedule."

"You'll have to rearrange it somehow, babe," Owen said with a grin. "I know you can do it. You can do anything you set your mind to, as you've so often reminded me."

Shelby could not believe this. He was leaving. "Owen. I said no. If you leave without Jake, I am going to call Judge Baker and tell him you're violating our custody arrangement."

"Are you nuts?"

"Joint custody means joint responsibility. You can't just dump a child on someone because he's inconvenient. You would howl at the moon if I did this to you."

Owen was already halfway out the door. "I spend as much time as you and the court will allow with my son. As I have repeatedly said, this is an important meeting. My whole career could hinge on this case, okay?"

Everything was always about Owen's career. She admitted defeat. Otherwise, he would keep her arguing here all night. "Fine," she said tightly. "When do you want to pick him up?"

"You can just leave him at day care tomorrow morning." He flashed that infuriating smile once again and slipped out the door before she could object. He didn't thank her or admit that she was doing him a favor. As usual, he just expected her to accommodate him.

Shelby tried calling Lori, but she didn't answer her cell. Next she tried First Strike. Gavin answered the phone.

"Hi, Gavin, it's Shelby Dorset. Is Lori there?" She did her best to inject a note of cool professionalism in her voice. But it was becoming increasingly difficult to maintain an impersonal distance where Gavin was concerned.

"She went with Beau to pick up an FTA. I expected them back before now."

An "FTA" was a "Failure to Appear," or a criminal suspect out on bail who hadn't shown up for his or her court hearing. Bail bondsmen hired bounty hunters to round up the strays and bring them back into the system. Lori had explained that FTAs were the bread and butter at First Strike, filling in the gaps between the big-money, high-profile cases. The bail bondsman next door provided them with lots of cases.

"I'm supposed to meet Lori in a few minutes," Shelby explained. "But I have my son with me now, sort of unexpected." Her voice wavered, and she was horrified to realize she was close to tears. But that was the effect Owen had on her. She was completely helpless in any sort of confrontation with him. He always got his way, and it infuriated her. Which made her cry.

"You okay, Ms. Dorset?" Gavin asked gently.

She took a deep breath. "I'm fine."

"Why don't you come anyway? I can keep an eye on your little boy while you ladies grapple."

That made her laugh. "You're offering to baby-sit?"

"Sure. I baby-sit for my little cousin all the time. I like kids. Of course, I'll understand if you don't want an ex-con watching your son."

"It's not that," she said hastily. Truth was, she just

wasn't up to being social tonight. Her confrontation with Owen had left her feeling wrung out. She wanted to crawl under the covers and not come out until daylight.

"Lori will be really disappointed if you don't show up," he said. "I don't know if you realize this, but Lori doesn't have much in the way of women friends."

"Why not?"

"I'm not sure. But I think she doesn't have much in common with most women."

"Or she intimidates the hell out of them," Shelby added, feeling a stab of sympathy for Lori. Shelby knew what it was like to not have friends. Her family's extreme wealth had set her apart from a lot of people. And the rich girls she normally would have socialized with didn't want anything to do with a bookish, gangly girl with thick glasses who was taller than the boys, a disaster at sports and a stutterer on top of everything else.

Thankfully the boys had caught up with her, height-wise, and her body had filled out. A speech therapist had cured her stuttering and laser surgery had eliminated the glasses. She was still a disaster at sports and would still rather spend her time with her nose in a book than socializing at a party. But those traits weren't such a liability anymore.

"I'll come for a little while," Shelby said. At least long enough to tell Lori she couldn't stay. A bounty hunters' den was no place for a three-year-old, and Owen would pitch a screaming fit if he found out about it, never mind it was his fault she'd been put in this difficult position.

Twenty minutes later as she parked her car in front of First Strike, she marveled at the fact that she was bringing her child into a neighborhood that had scared the pants off her just a month ago, and into an office that had repulsed her. But Gavin and his co-workers had straightened up the office. At least the distasteful magazines and beer bottles had disappeared, and there was no longer a jockstrap on the workout machine. Someone had run a vacuum cleaner, and the place smelled better. Shelby had spotted a couple of Glade PlugIns on her last visit.

As for safety, well, Paulie Sapp could have kidnapped her anywhere. Still, she took a good look around her before she got out of the car, then opened the back and unstrapped Jake from his car seat.

Lights blazed inside the First Strike office. Through the front window, which had actually been cleaned, she could see Gavin sitting at his desk talking on the phone. He had his chair back, his feet up on the desk.

She paused a few seconds to admire him. Lord, he could make a woman drool. Those snug, faded jeans, those shoulders. Even his big, strong hands as they held the phone receiver in an easy grip, made her think of things she shouldn't.

"Down, girl," she murmured, opening the door. He looked over, smiled and waved, held up a finger to indicate he'd be with her in a minute and continued his conversation.

"The Kyle Nelson I'm looking for went to Thomas Edison High," Gavin said easily. "Yeah, he was my best friend back then."

Jake was squirming, so Shelby put him down so he could explore. Of course, this office wasn't anywhere near childproof, so she followed him around to make sure he didn't get into trouble.

"Yeah, Johnny Hobbs!" Gavin said. "Except I go by John now. Can you have him call me?" He rattled off a number that wasn't one Shelby recognized and hung up.

She shook her head. "As your parole officer, I officially frown on that pack of lies you just told." Then she grinned. "But I admire your technique."

"Hey, Ms. Dorset. Lori's on her way. It took her a little longer to process the FTA than she'd planned on."

"That's okay. This is my son, Jake. Jake, this is Mr. Schuyler."

Jake had already stopped investigating a canister full of pens to stare wide-eyed at Gavin.

"Hi, Jake," Gavin said. "Whassup?" He didn't speak to Jake the way most adults did. He didn't talk baby talk, and he didn't stare. He just talked.

Amazingly, instead of hiding behind Shelby's leg the way he usually did around strangers, Jake ran right up to Gavin. "Daddy went to a meetin'."

"What kind of meeting?" Gavin asked, as if he were really interested.

"Mmm, a fancy one. With a lady."

Shelby's scalp tingled. A fancy meeting with a lady? Okay, well, his big client could be a lady.

"He wore his *blue* underwear," Jake added. "Blue underwear is for fancy meetings. What's in here?" He opened a drawer in Gavin's desk. "Ohhh!" Sounded like he'd found treasure. He pulled out a legal pad.

"He loves to draw and color," Shelby said, still reeling from Jake's revelation. Blue underwear? The flush started at her scalp and worked its way down.

"Then I have just the thing," Gavin said, though he cast a worried look at Shelby, who was trying mightily to swallow down the tightness in her throat.

Gavin led Jake to the back of the office and some storage cabinets. From one of the cabinets he produced a huge pad of white paper—must have been two feet by four feet.

"Wow!" Jake was suitably impressed.

Gavin took the pad of paper to an empty corner and put it on the floor. Then he produced a handful of colored markers. "It's for planning any really big extraction," Gavin explained to Shelby. "If a fugitive is holed up in a building, they'll draw maps and plot out who goes where, so everybody knows their job."

Jake pounced on the pad of paper and markers. He spread out the colors in a line, carefully choosing which one he would use first.

"That's interesting," Shelby said, determined to distract herself from her dark, angry thoughts. "How— I mean, who—" But it was no good. "Owen is a tighty-whity man all the way," she blurted out.

"Oh," Gavin said, obviously grasping the significance.

She wanted to vent. Really bad. But one, she'd promised herself she would never bad-mouth Owen in front of Jake, no matter how richly he deserved it. Second, she couldn't reveal anything so intensely personal to Gavin, with whom she was supposed to have a strictly professional relationship.

"Listen, I need to just step outside for a few minutes, okay?"

"Not out there, not by yourself. Ms. Dorset…Shelby. It's okay. If I've got this figured out, you just learned something that's bound to upset you. You're entitled to have a hissy fit. I'll just go over here and help Jake draw a picture."

"I'm not upset about him dating," Shelby said. "We're divorced. We've been divorced for two years. He's already had a half-dozen girlfriends, and other than concern about the influence that might have on J-a-k-e, I don't care. I'm mad because he lied to me. This is his week to have custody of…you know, but he thinks nothing of inconveniencing me, because nothing I do is as important as what he does, even if it's a hot date with some bimbo." She glanced at Jake, but he seemed to be entranced with his artwork.

"If it really was an important meeting that came up suddenly, I'd be irritated but I'd try to be understanding. But for a *date?* And he didn't even ask. He just barged into my house, dropped Jake off and pretended he didn't hear me when I said, 'No, you cannot do this to me, it's not fair. It's not what we agreed to.' Yet if I'm ten minutes late dropping Jake off, he's on the phone to our divorce judge making a complaint."

Oh, God. She was standing there in the middle of the office, her face hot, her throat thick, pouring out her misery to Gavin Schuyler, of all people. She didn't know what to say, what to do next. She was paralyzed.

He'd moved closer to her, though he was still a couple of feet away. "I won't think any less of you if you want to cry. You can go into the bathroom."

She wasn't going to make it to the bathroom. Great, heaving sobs welled up from somewhere deep inside her. She had no idea why here, why now. It shouldn't be that big a deal that Owen had lied to her and manipulated her. Hell, he'd done it throughout their whole marriage. This was nothing new.

She clamped her hand over her mouth, but it didn't help. Tears dripped out of her eyes and her nose stopped up and she had to breathe through her mouth, terrible gasps. She didn't want Jake to see her like this. She didn't want *anyone* to see her fall apart. But she couldn't seem to stop herself.

She could tell Gavin wanted to touch her, to comfort her, but he wasn't going to cross that boundary. He'd shown from the beginning he was keenly aware of the professional and social barriers between them. Hell, he wouldn't even call her by her first name before now— and he'd saved her life!

Right now, Shelby didn't give a damn about propriety and professionalism. At the moment, she had none. Nothing to preserve. Gavin wasn't going to touch her unless she touched him first. So she did. She reached out and grabbed a handful of his nubbly sweater.

That was all it took. Gavin folded her into his arms. She pressed her face against his shoulder to muffle herself, then let her racking sobs take over.

He held her gently, respectfully. "You'll feel better in a few minutes. Just let 'er rip."

She did. She cried as she hadn't cried since the day she'd moved out of the pretty little house she and Owen had shared, and which he'd gotten in their settlement.

"I don't know what's wrong with me," she said when she could talk. She was clinging to Gavin, unable to let him go.

"It's probably been building up," Gavin said reasonably, apparently not uncomfortable with her tears. He patted her back reassuringly. "You've had a pretty stressful few weeks."

"Or maybe I'm just cracking up."

"A man killed himself in front of you. Then you almost got killed yourself. You probably didn't cry after either of those things."

No, she hadn't, she realized.

"So, it's just catching up with you. Give yourself a break."

She wanted to believe Gavin. She would much rather believe she was suffering from a delayed reaction to the violence she'd been part of, than admit that Owen had this much power over her.

She glanced around Gavin's shoulder at Jake. He lay on his side, his head pillowed against one arm, drawing big purple circles on his giant paper. She thought at first he wasn't paying her any attention. Then he glanced her way, almost furtively.

"Your mom's okay," she called to him. Reluctantly, she pulled away from Gavin. He released her instantly. "I'm so embarrassed."

"For being human?"

"I'm your parole officer. I'm not supposed to act like this."

He rolled his eyes. "You're not a robot. I'll forget this ever happened, okay? We won't ever mention it. Everything will be exactly like it was before."

That seemed reasonable. Problem was, Shelby didn't want to go back to the way it had been before. She'd liked the feel of his arms around her just a little too much. She'd liked it when he called her "Shelby" instead of "Ms. Dorset."

"First thing tomorrow morning, I'm going to have you reassigned to a different parole officer," she said, her voice still shaky. "Clearly I can't maintain professional distance with you anymore."

"Aw, Shelby, you don't want to go and do that. I like you. I don't want to have to go breaking in a new parole officer when we're getting along so well."

"We're getting along *too* well," she mumbled.

"I'll be good. No more touching. I'll go back to calling you Ms. Dorset."

"I'm sorry, Gavin, but my mind's made up. Being a parole officer isn't a job that earns a lot of respect or monetary rewards. I need my self-respect, which means I can't compromise my ethics. I'll make sure you get someone nice," she added, thinking that if she could get Ramona to agree, Rosie would finally get her wish.

"Well, if you're sure."

"I am."

"In that case…"

She didn't know how it happened, but suddenly he was kissing her. And she was definitely kissing him back. His mouth was sure and confident on hers, taking command, leaving her weak-kneed and dizzy with sudden need. His arms were around her, holding her prisoner—holding her upright, if truth be known, because she would have dropped like a stone if he'd let her go, she was so light-headed.

Excited but terrified at the line they'd crossed, Shelby reached up one tentative hand. She'd always wanted to touch his hair, which looked so thick and soft and dark as crows' feathers. It was soft, and she buried her hand in it, clinging to the collar of his sweater with the other hand.

A noise coming from the back of the office startled her. Gavin tensed, too, and they reluctantly pulled apart. She stumbled slightly until she recovered her equilibrium, and Gavin held on to her arm until he was sure she wouldn't fall.

"I'm not up for explanations," Shelby said apologetically.

"Me, neither." He gave her a conspiratorial smile. She quickly wiped some of her lipstick off his face. Then she scurried over to see what Jake was doing. She hoped he hadn't seen her kissing Gavin. Knowing Jake, he would tell Owen all about it. He had a keen memory and a darn good vocabulary.

One good thing, she thought dazedly. She was no longer angry at Owen. She simply didn't have room for that many emotions in her brain, and her confused feelings for what had just happened between her and Gavin had won out.

Lori emerged from the kitchenette, her face flushed from the cold. "Shelby, I'm so sorry I'm late. I got stuck at the police station processing a guy. They couldn't find his records. Some computer glitch."

"It's okay," Shelby said.

Lori skidded to a stop when she saw Jake. She flashed a tentative smile. "Your son, I take it?"

"Yeah. My ex dropped him on me unexpectedly. We should probably reschedule our self-defense lesson."

Lori approached cautiously. Unlike most women Shelby knew, Lori didn't immediately gush all over Jake. She studied him from a safe distance, as if he were an alien species. "He's how old?"

"Three. Big for his age, though."

"He doesn't look much like you."

"He favors his father, who fortunately is a handsome man. Let's just hope he didn't inherit his sire's more unfavorable traits." There. She'd said it in a way Jake wouldn't understand, thereby keeping her pledge not to tear Owen down in front of Jake.

"I'm finished, Mommy," he said, proudly showing her his work of art.

"Very nice," Shelby said. "Is it…an elephant?"

"No. It's Daddy's house, with the tree and the flowers."

Formerly Shelby's house, too. She'd planted those azaleas herself. Not that her tidy, modern condo with its big kitchen skylight wasn't comfortable. But sometimes she missed all the space she used to have. "Oh, now I see." She ripped the page out of the huge pad and rolled it up for safekeeping.

"I can watch him for a while," Gavin said, "if you two want to beat up on each other."

"You just want to watch us wrestle," Lori said.

Gavin shrugged. "Maybe."

"I need to get Jake some dinner," Shelby said.

"McDonald's!" Jake shouted excitedly.

"Not today." Jake got enough fast food, which was all his father fed him. "We'll go home, and Mommy will fix you something yummy." She picked him up, needing to get out of there. Needing to put some distance between herself and Gavin.

"Want to try again tomorrow?" Lori asked.

"Sure, that would be great." Shelby found her purse. "Have a good evening."

"I'll walk you to your car," Gavin said, and she couldn't very well argue against it. It was dark now, and even in the best of circumstances she'd become uneasy getting into her car since the thwarted kidnapping. "We need to talk," he said once they were outside.

"It was just a kiss," she said, trying to sound offhand.

"Not about that. About Paulie Sapp."

She froze. "Oh, hell, Gavin, you didn't—"

"Of course I didn't. But haven't you been wondering what I was doing at his apartment in the first place?"

She'd been trying very hard *not* to think about it. Once she'd learned Gavin had been cleared as a suspect, she'd put it out of her mind. "I've been trying really hard to overlook the fact you were in the company of a known felon," she said quietly. "That does violate your parole. Or it would have if he hadn't been dead by the time you got there. But I know you went over there in some misguided attempt to protect me, to warn him away from me or something. I appreciate it, I really do, but it wasn't the best decision you've ever made. Given how well you've been doing otherwise, I wasn't going to say anything."

"I was going over there to question him, since it's obvious Palmer won't follow up. I found out something about Sapp that concerned me…" He hesitated.

"Let's sit in the car where it's warmer," she said, opening the back door to put Jake in his car seat. She gave him his favorite truck to play with, hoping it would satisfy him for a few minutes. Then she and Gavin climbed in front. She switched on the engine and adjusted the heater. Neither she nor Jake wore a coat, but it felt as if a front had moved in. Her teeth chattered.

"I'm not sure how you'll take this. It may be nothing. But I found a connection between Manny Cruz and Paulie Sapp."

"Really? What?"

"They both know your ex-husband."

Shelby took a moment to absorb what he'd said. "Are you saying you think Owen is somehow involved in all this?"

"Ex-spouses make handy suspects, I know. But any good cop would at least consider the possibility. Unfortunately, Palmer's not a good cop. I was just going to lean on Sapp a little, see if he might tell me who wanted him to kidnap you. He lied about you being his parole officer. So something else had to be behind the crime."

"Owen would never want to harm me," she said flatly. "He has nothing to gain."

"Full custody of Jake?"

"He doesn't want that." Owen already resented the time he had to spend with Jake. It put a crimp in his lifestyle—as tonight demonstrated. "Plus, I pay him child support. He would lose that if I—if I was out of the picture."

"Would Jake inherit?"

"I don't have much money of my own. I have a trust, but Owen would never be able to get his hands on it, even if I, you know. No, he wouldn't want me gone. Besides, Owen might be a j-e-r-k, but he's not *that* much of one. I don't believe he's capable of m-u-r-d-e-r."

"Does he have money problems?"

"Probably. He always spent more than he made."

"Sapp said he wanted to hold you for ransom. Maybe Owen was planning to bleed your family."

Shelby forced herself to consider the possibility. Then she shook her head. "No. I just don't think so. Does Craig have any leads on Paulie Sapp's murder?"

Gavin shrugged. "I'm not exactly in the loop."

"Gavin, promise me you won't get further involved in this. It's noble of you to worry about me, and I know as a former cop you're itching to solve the mystery. But it's best if you stay out of it."

"I believe you could be in danger—if not from O-w-e-n, then from some other nutcase who knows your family has money."

"I'm being careful."

Gavin sighed. "All right. Now, about that k-i-s-s…"

Chapter Six

Gavin knew he was pressing his luck. But he had to know where he stood with Shelby. It might have been a mistake, kissing her like that. But she hadn't exactly pushed him away.

The expression on her face was hardly encouraging. She wouldn't even look at him.

"You're going to say it was a mistake," he concluded.

"No, not a mistake. Maybe we both needed to know…what it would be like."

"And now we can move on?"

"Exactly," she said, seemingly pleased that he understood.

"So you've always wanted to kiss an ex-con, is that it?"

"No, of course not," she said hotly. "You make it sound like some fetish, like I go around panting after all my clients, that I lie in bed at night fantasizing about taking a walk on the wild side."

"You don't?"

"I did fantasize about kissing you," she admitted, her brief burst of temper spent. "But not because you're an ex-con."

He'd fantasized about more than kissing. But he didn't suppose now was the time to bring that up.

From the back seat, Jake made truck noises, thankfully absorbed in his play.

Hell, this was crazy. Shelby reminded him of Marcie Kimball, the cheerleader he'd had a crush on in high school. He'd finally made out with her in the back seat of her dad's Mercedes, and he'd discovered she was as hot for him as he was for her—but only when they were alone. She wouldn't go out with him. She wouldn't be seen in public with him, and in fact ignored him if any of her snooty friends were around.

"I guess it wouldn't work anyway." He'd wanted to be the first to say it.

"Owen was my walk on the wild side. He was poor and he had long hair and rode a motorcycle, and he was someone my parents hated. He had a wild, defiant streak—he didn't care what anybody thought. He was the most exciting thing to ever happen to me. But he was such a mistake. Such a big, huge mistake. Jakey was the only good thing to come of it."

"So, no more bad boys?"

"That's my motto."

"Gonna marry someone safe and boring next time, huh?"

"If I ever marry again, it will be to someone safe and boring, yes. Someone like me. The only thing Owen and I had in common was a misguided desire to save the world, an ideal he abandoned pretty quickly once he encountered the realities of a law career."

"But you still want to save the world," Gavin concluded.

"Only little parts of it."

That was what he admired about her.

"Gavin, if I became involved with an ex-con, Owen would sue me for custody so fast my head would spin. He would probably get it, too. I'm not concerned about your being around Jake. I know you're basically a good person despite your past mistakes. But the rest of the world might not see it that way."

And that was one argument he couldn't refute. Where her son was concerned, Shelby wouldn't take any chances.

"I understand," he finally said. "Promise me you'll be careful."

"You know I will. Oh, Gavin. Before you leave, there's something on the floor in the back seat for you."

Puzzled, he reached between the front seats and felt around until he discovered a long, narrow package wrapped in white paper. "What's this?"

"A belated housewarming present. Don't open it here. I'm a little embarrassed."

"You didn't have to do that, but thanks." He maneuvered the long package into the front and out the door with him as he left her.

Lori was already gone by the time Gavin went back into the office. He closed up, made sure the answering machine was on, then headed out the back door and up to his loft. Once inside, he ripped the package open, burning with curiosity.

It was a rug, a big, furry, purple-and-white throw rug, the perfect size for a bare stretch of wood floor in his bedroom area. He spread it reverently onto the floor, then just stared at it. That was just about the nicest, most thoughtful gift anyone had ever given him.

"SHELBY, YOU'RE A TRUE FRIEND." Rosie stood at the entrance to Shelby's cubicle, beaming. "But I can't believe you gave him up. He's such a hottie."

Shelby was eating lunch at her desk, a slice of vending-machine pizza, which was perhaps one of the most disgusting foods on earth. But she'd overslept this morning and hadn't had time to fix a sack lunch.

Rosie was holding her own lunch, a beef burrito from the same vending machine.

Shelby summoned a smile for her friend. "Sit down. We can ingest a three-day supply of grease together. So I take it Ramona gave you the news."

Rosie grabbed the chair across from Shelby and set down her lunch and a can of Diet Coke. "But Ramona wouldn't tell me why you wanted to get rid of him. Well, she said something about 'friction,' I think." She gave Shelby a wink.

"Not that kind of friction. I just didn't feel comfortable with him anymore," she said in a speech she'd rehearsed over and over in her head last night, which explained why she'd overslept. "When he saved my life, it changed the balance of power between us. I didn't feel like I could be an effective authority figure once he'd seen me sprawled on the street with blood all over my face." The explanation had worked for Ramona.

But Rosie knew Shelby better than almost anyone. She studied Shelby now with a shrewd eye. "There's something you're not telling me. Oh, come on, Shelby, what really happened? I need to know, right? Did he come on to you? Did you come on to him?"

Shelby wanted to deny it. But she had a hard time

telling an out-and-out lie to Rosie. "There is some chemistry," she admitted. "And that's part of the problem."

"Ah-hah, I knew it! You're just so darn ethical. It wouldn't be a problem for me."

"You say that, but you wouldn't actually sleep with one of the guys you supervise, would you?"

Rosie hesitated.

"You haven't, have you? Rosie, that's sexual harassment."

"All right, all right. No, I've never slept with a parolee. And no, I probably wouldn't ever do that. But I've never had one as cute as Gavin Schuyler, either. A little chemistry with him certainly wouldn't send me running for the hills."

"It's not just that. I've become friends with one of his co-workers, which in turn makes me sort of friends with him. I couldn't be objective anymore. Technically he shouldn't have been anywhere near Paulie Sapp, who's a known felon. But I didn't call him on it."

Rosie frowned. "*I* won't have to turn him in for that, will I? You know how Ramona is. By the book all the way."

"Ramona doesn't think it's necessary, given the circumstances. But the last thing I did as Gavin's parole officer was warn him not to do any more investigating on his own. He's to stick to the cases he gets at work. Phone work and surveillance only, no face-to-face contact with suspects."

Rosie looked relieved. She took a big bite of her deep-fried burrito, which gave a satisfying crunch, then washed it down with cola. "Hey, you're helping me move tomorrow, right?"

"You bet. You want me to bring anything? Cleaning products, paper towels?"

"Um, some glass cleaner, maybe," Rosie said. "And could you stop at Krispy Kreme on your way over and get us some doughnuts? I sort of bribed some friends and relatives with the promise of all the Krispy Kreme doughnuts they could eat."

"Sure, I can do that."

SHELBY YAWNED as she pulled into the parking lot of a large supermarket at seven forty-five Saturday morning. Her eyes were gritty from lack of sleep, but she was glad to have something to occupy her weekend. She would get Jake again on Monday after work, and her little man would be hers again for a whole week. Just long enough to work out all the bad habits Owen instilled in him, like no bedtime, no baths and a steady diet of Happy Meals.

Meanwhile, her place was too empty, too quiet, with too much time to brood. Memories of Manny Cruz's suicide sometimes jumped into her consciousness without warning if she sat idle too long.

Krispy Kreme was next to the supermarket, and she could smell the warm, yeasty doughnuts even in her closed car. Her stomach growled.

All the parking spaces near the door were taken, so she pulled into a space out in the lot. She ran into the grocery store to buy glass cleaner, then dashed next door and bought an array of four dozen doughnuts.

As she headed back out into the parking lot, she didn't immediately see her car, then realized a huge white truck had parked next to her, blocking her view.

He had the whole parking lot to choose from, she thought. Why'd he have to park right next to her?

She headed toward her car, unlocking it with the remote on her key chain, when she noticed a cop standing by her back bumper, looking right at her. He was tall and lanky with a buzz haircut and a pointy chin.

She felt a chill of alarm until he smiled. "Hello, ma'am. I'm sorry to be the bearer of bad news, but someone just hit your car and drove away. My partner's chasing down the driver."

"My car?"

"The damage is mostly to the right rear-quarter panel. It's not too bad."

She stepped around to where he indicated. The car looked fine to her. She was just about to ask the cop what in the world he was talking about when he grabbed her from behind and pressed a cloth over her nose and mouth.

Chloroform, she realized, struggling against her attacker. But he was strong, and she quickly weakened. Her vision narrowed to a tunnel, then a pinpoint, then everything went black.

She woke up in what felt like seconds to find herself lying in a dark place on a hard metal surface. She was on her stomach, her hands wrenched behind her, her mouth taped. Her feet were tied, and her attacker was busy tying her hands.

She could see a sliver of light near the floor. She was in the back of that white truck, she realized. This was a well-planned, well-executed kidnapping.

She screamed ineffectually and tried to roll out from under the man, which of course she couldn't do. He was far stronger than she was.

He said absolutely nothing, moving with almost clinical precision, as if he'd done this a time or two.

Shelby ordered her sluggish brain to think, to observe, to remember. Was anything in the truck besides her and the man? Anything to use as a weapon or a means of escape?

She saw the boxes of doughnuts, some of them spilled out onto the floor of the truck; the plastic bag with window cleaner and her leather purse. These were things a professional wouldn't leave at the scene, so it wouldn't look like an obvious abduction.

Was there anything in her purse? Hell, why hadn't she listened to Gavin about getting a gun? Her only possible weapon was her key chain. It had been in her hand when the guy grabbed her. Where was it now? She didn't see it.

She tried desperately to remember some technique Lori had taught her for a situation like this. Unfortunately, the time to use such techniques would have been when the guy first grabbed her, not now, when he had her trussed up like a calf at a rodeo. But she'd been paralyzed by shock at first. And the chloroform had taken effect so quickly, she simply hadn't had time to do anything.

Now, the only part of her body she could move was her feet. She swung them up and hit her abductor in his back with a satisfying thump.

"Hey, knock it off," he objected, and he backhanded her face.

Her eyes watered and her nose burned. She'd never been hit in the face before, and she'd had no idea it would hurt so much. And, hell, the guy hadn't even been trying. It had been like swatting a fly for him.

She sobbed at the hopelessness of it all.

The man finally got off her, satisfied she was securely tied. He opened the truck door wider, checked to make sure no one was watching, then rolled out. The truck door slammed shut with a resounding clank, leaving her in almost total darkness. She heard it lock.

Oh, God, she was going to die. Why hadn't she taken Gavin's warnings more seriously? Because she hadn't really believed him. She didn't believe for a minute Owen could be behind something so evil, so the fact he had tenuous connections to both of the ex-cons who'd assaulted her had meant little. After all, he was connected to most of the criminals in the county.

She should have listened. Gavin had been a cop, and a good one before his downfall. He obviously still had instincts.

It was hard to think clearly, to push aside her own terror and misery, but she forced herself to do it. What tools did she have at her disposal?

Her purse. And her cell phone. Yes, her cell phone! Unless that troglodyte had taken it.

The truck's engine started up. Shelby paid careful attention to which way it turned, so she could at least make an educated guess as to her location.

She pushed herself onto her knees. Her balance was precarious, and when the truck turned out of the parking lot she fell over. But she soon righted herself and scooted along the floor of the truck until she nudged her purse with her knee.

The truck made a left. Ryder Road? Ryder was a bumpy two-lane currently being resurfaced. She'd had to stop for construction on the way to the doughnut shop.

The truck accelerated, and the surface seemed smooth. No stops. Must be Valley Glen, then.

First she had to get the tape off her mouth. Fortunately her attacker hadn't paid much attention when he'd slapped the tape over her mouth, probably figuring that he only needed to keep her silent until he had her in the truck. She'd been unconscious, her mouth slack, and the piece of tape wasn't very large. She pushed her tongue against the tape and around her lips until she pried one edge up. If she could just get hold of that edge somehow and yank…

She raked off both of her slip-on loafers. Then she maneuvered to a sitting position, her legs in front of her. By leaning between her knees, she could get her mouth close to her feet. She'd always been limber, and the sporadic yoga classes she took made her even more flexible. She maneuvered the loose edge of tape between her big toes, then sat up.

The first two times she tried it, the tape slipped out from between her toes. But each time, a bit more tape peeled away from her mouth. On her third try, she got a really good grip on the sticky surface and yanked her head back.

The skin around her mouth stung, but she was free of the gag.

She twisted around until she could grab her purse with her bound hands. She got the zipper open. She felt around until she located the cell phone. Yes! She opened it and pressed the power button. It beeped to life.

Only one problem. With her hands behind her, she couldn't see the display. She wanted to dial 9-1-1, but there were so many buttons, and she wasn't sure she could hit the right ones by feel alone. If she misdialed, she might never recover. She might not get a call out at all.

But she knew where the redial button was. Lower left. Who was the last person she'd called? The First Strike Agency, when she'd talked to Lori yesterday. But would anyone be there at the crack of dawn on a Saturday morning?

She decided to risk it. If nothing else, she could leave a message on the answering machine. Then she could hang up, turn the phone off, turn it on again and try for 9-1-1.

She pushed redial. Then she balanced the open phone against her purse and turned around, bending low to get her mouth close to the phone so she could hear and be heard.

It was ringing. Then someone answered.

"First Strike Agency."

"Gavin?"

"Shelby? Hi." He sounded pleased to hear from her. "Lori's not—"

"Don't talk, just listen. I've been kidnapped. I'm in a big white truck with no markings. I think I'm heading east on Valley Glen—"

Just then the truck made a sharp right turn. Shelby's purse tipped over. The phone rolled and bounced across the truck's floor. The greenish light from the LCD blinked out.

Oh, God. She scooted laboriously across the truck floor in the direction she believed the phone had gone. When she finally found it, she picked it up again. But no amount of button pushing would bring the phone back to life.

Had Gavin heard her? Had he understood?

The truck pulled to a stop. It sat in one place, idling for a long time. Shelby could barely make out the sound of a train signal. Now she knew exactly where she was. Sometimes the trains that came through here were very long and very slow. They might be stuck here for several minutes! That was good news, but only if Gavin had gotten the message.

GAVIN STARED at the dead phone receiver, perplexed. He'd been talking to Shelby on her cell phone, that much he knew. And she'd sounded upset, but he hadn't been able to make out most of the words because the connection had cut in and out, and she'd sounded kind of far away, as if she didn't have the phone close enough to her mouth.

Something about a white truck heading east on Valley Glen.

Then he remembered she'd said something about helping her friend Rosie move today. Rosie, his new parole officer. Had they broken down or had a wreck?

Hell, if Shelby needed help, there was no way he could ignore the summons, even if she'd as much as told him he wasn't good enough for her. And she'd given him that damn rug, which made him think of her every single time he saw it or walked on it.

He went out the back way, locked the door, then climbed into his '74 Barracuda. The car had been his grandmother's. When Aubrey had moved into their granny's house after her death, the car was still in the garage. The family had never gotten around to selling it. It hadn't been driven in years, but Gavin had spent a few weekends working on it right after his release from prison. Hell, those auto-shop vocational classes he'd taken in prison had come in handy.

Now it was a real cream puff. Needed a paint job, but it ran like a bat out of hell.

When he reached Valley Glen, he turned east. At the railroad crossing, he encountered a long line of cars waiting for a train to pass. Toward the front of the line was a large white truck, no markings. Maybe that was it. But it looked to be fully operational.

As soon as traffic started to move again, Gavin got into the left lane and worked his way closer to the truck, then pulled up even with it.

A man he didn't recognize was behind the wheel. He wore a beige City of Payton cop's uniform, except something was definitely wrong with that uniform. It had captain's stripes on the sleeves. Gavin knew every captain on the force, at least by sight. This guy wasn't one. He wasn't even old enough to be a captain.

Gavin dropped back and followed at a discreet distance, not wanting to alert the fake cop of his presence until he had a plan in place.

Shelby was in that truck. He could almost feel her presence. She'd called to let him know she'd been kidnapped yet again. She'd called him, not the cops. She'd trusted him to save her life as he'd done before, and he damn well wasn't going to disappoint her.

Adrenaline surged through his veins, sharpening his mind. He could stop someplace and call for reinforcements. But if he did that, he chanced losing the truck, and that wasn't an option.

He followed for a couple of minutes, hoping the truck

might stop. But as Valley Glenn turned into a rural road, traffic thinned. Gavin would not be able to follow for long without attracting the truck driver's attention.

He had to make a move.

Valley Glenn, now Highway 2021, had petered into a two-lane country road. Gavin slid the passenger window down and pulled the Barracuda into the oncoming lane, which was empty, thank God.

The fake cop was looking right at him. Gavin motioned for him to roll his window down. He intended to tell the truck driver he had a flat tire.

The man didn't react as Gavin had hoped. Instead, he veered the truck directly into Gavin's lane, violently bumping the Barracuda.

The maniac was trying to run him off the road! Gavin hit the gas and straightened out his car. He wanted to pull ahead of the truck, maybe block his way somehow and force him to stop.

He didn't have a weapon, and he had no idea whether the truck's driver was armed. But it was a safe bet if he'd kidnapped Shelby. This might be suicide. But, damn it, he wasn't going to let this guy drive off without a fight. The truck driver's irrational behavior only strengthened Gavin's belief that he did, indeed, have Shelby in the truck.

He pulled ahead of the truck, but the large, lumbering vehicle had more get-up-and-go than Gavin had counted on. It surged forward and crashed into his bumper, sending the Barracuda into a fishtail.

Gavin managed to get control of his huge car. Rather than let the guy bump him again, he moved back into the opposite lane and slammed on the brakes, intending to return to his position behind the truck. In a contest of sheer brute force the truck would win. But if he simply continued to follow it, well, it would have to stop some time. It couldn't outrun him. And Gavin had a full tank of gas.

Unfortunately, the truck didn't let him pull in behind. The driver slammed on his brakes, too, and made a hard left with the steering wheel. The truck bashed into the Barracuda's passenger door and sent it careening toward the opposite shoulder.

Gavin tried to regain control of the car, but the inertia pulling it off the road was too great a force to overcome. The car went right into the ditch, rolled over half a turn, and landed on its roof.

Fortunately, the old car was a massively heavy hunk of steel. It didn't crush. Thanks to his seat belt, Gavin was completely unhurt. He unfastened the belt. The door wouldn't open, but he was able to crawl out the open passenger window.

It was only when he was out of the car, standing upright and cursing his luck, that he realized the truck hadn't escaped from the accident unscathed. The driver had apparently lost control, too. The truck was fifty or so yards up the road, off on the shoulder, sitting in some tall weeds. The engine was straining to start, rolling over and over and over, but it wouldn't catch.

Gavin dashed across the road, then sprinted toward the truck, hoping he was out of the driver's line of vision.

When he reached the truck, he didn't think too hard about what he had to do. That engine might catch any second, and the truck would be gone. The ditch wasn't as deep on this side of the road. So Gavin just ran straight up to the driver's door and jerked it open, counting on the fact that most people didn't lock their doors while they were driving.

He was right. The fake cop looked plenty surprised to see Gavin there, and even more surprised when Gavin grabbed an arm and hauled him out of the truck. That was when Gavin noticed the truck had a passenger. He had only a fleeting impression of the person, enough to know it wasn't Shelby. Two against one—his odds of prevailing had just plummeted.

The driver's state of surprise didn't last long. He landed on his feet like a cat and immediately went on the attack.

Gavin was ready. In addition to his police training, he'd picked up a few dirty tricks in prison—anything to get the upper hand.

His opponent was an inch or two taller than Gavin but skinny. Still, he was no stranger to fighting. With his longer arms, he got in a couple of face punches right away, sneaking in from above, before Gavin could figure out how to block him.

Gavin landed a kick to the guy's gut, which slowed him down a fraction. He tried to cash in on the small advantage, launching another kick, blocking a feeble strike to his face. The fake cop was breathing heavily, his face red, his expression one of pure rage.

Gavin breathed hard, too, but he still had a lot of energy, courtesy of his adrenaline rush. He thought he might have a fitness advantage over his opponent, too. In prison, Gavin had run endless miles in place in his cell to strengthen his injured leg and performed hundreds and hundreds of push-ups. The very first day he was free, he'd gone for a run—amazed when he realized he'd run seven miles. He'd kept it up, too. He ran every morning. It only took a quarter mile to work the stiffness out of his right thigh.

If he could just get this guy down on the ground…

The other man suddenly backed up, retreating around the front of the truck.

Yeah, that would work, too, getting him to run away. If the chicken SOB would just take off across that peach orchard, Gavin could focus on the passenger, who was apparently cowering inside the truck, unwilling to jump into the fray.

Or he might be loading a gun.

He heard a muffled thumping and realized it was coming from inside the truck. Shelby! He wanted to tell her he was here, offer her some reassurance. She must be terrified. But he couldn't afford to take his focus off his opponent.

Determined to remain on the offensive, Gavin charged around the front of the truck. He came around the corner just in time to see his opponent swinging a huge piece of scrap metal—some part of the truck that had fallen off, or something that had been lying conveniently in the grass.

Gavin tried to dodge the blow, but he wasn't quite fast enough. The truck's bumper—that's what it was— caught him squarely on his bad leg, which crumpled beneath him.

White-hot pain exploded in his leg and shot through every cell in his body, literally blinding him. Then another blow came, and that was the last thing he remembered.

Chapter Seven

Shelby was dying to know what was happening. The truck had gone through some reckless maneuvers, tossing her around in the back like a roulette marble. Then it had felt as if the truck went off the road. It had stopped abruptly, tilted at an awkward angle. The truck's driver tried to start it up again, but the engine wouldn't catch.

"Good," she said out loud. She was better off stranded on some highway, where a passerby might stop to help, than wherever this insane man wanted to take her.

She'd already slipped her shoes back on, in case she had to run. Now she lay on her back and beat on the side of the truck with her feet, in case someone did stop.

The truck had been stopped about five minutes when the rear door rattled. Someone was unfastening the lock.

She scooted toward the truck's rear. And when she couldn't move fast enough, she rolled. Then she poised herself on her back, knees in toward her chest, ready to kick the ever-lovin' snot out of this guy. She couldn't exactly run away with her feet tied, but if she could roll out of the truck, maybe someone would see her.

The door rolled open about six inches and a malevolent face peered in at her. "Get back."

She said nothing. Why should she obey him? She intended to make life as difficult as possible for her kidnapper, for as long as she was able.

A metal pole snaked its way inside the door and poked her on the hip. With a yelp she jumped about a foot off the bed of the truck and instinctively rolled to get away from this new threat. He'd hit her with a cattle prod! It felt as if she'd been smacked with a hammer. Her whole leg vibrated with the aftereffects of the shock.

As she tried to recover, the door opened wider and a man's inert body was unceremoniously dumped onto the truck floor.

"Gavin!" His face was covered in blood, and he was frighteningly still. Tears sprang to her eyes. He'd understood her terrified S.O.S., and he'd come to rescue her. For his trouble, he'd gotten himself beat up and taken prisoner…or worse.

The door slammed shut again, plunging them into darkness.

"Gavin, oh, Gavin, this is all my fault. I'll never forgive myself if I got you killed." She couldn't help him with her hands tied, but she just kept saying his name over and over, hoping to get some response.

She put her ear close to his face. She thought maybe he was breathing, but the truck engine was grinding again and she couldn't hear very well.

Shelby prayed the engine wouldn't catch. If their kidnapper had to get roadside help, the chance of his crime being discovered increased. Likewise if he tried to change vehicles.

Then the engine roared to life, and she cursed.

Gavin groaned. *Oh, thank heaven.* He was alive.

"Gavin! Don't try to move. You're injured."

"Shelby?" His voice was thick.

"You were hit in the head. You may have other injuries."

The truck rocked back and forth as it struggled to get out of the shallow ditch it had settled in. Shelby prayed again that the truck would be stuck, but after a few moments it lumbered out of the ditch and back onto the road.

"Damn," she muttered. "We can't catch a break here."

GAVIN'S HEAD FELT AS IF, well, exactly as if it had been hit by a truck bumper. He for sure had a concussion, but he didn't think it was any more serious than that. His leg ached but it wasn't broken. "How long was I out?" he asked, still a bit muzzy.

"Two or three minutes, maybe," Shelby said.

He pushed himself up into a sitting position, continuing to assess the physical damage. He probed his scalp with his fingers. "What about you?" he asked. "Are you injured?"

"No, he hasn't hurt me, except to zap me with a cattle prod."

"Damn. I didn't understand your phone call. I thought you'd broken down. I should have known…"

"No, Gavin, don't blame yourself. I'm the one who screwed up. You told me to be careful. I saw that cop's uniform and I completely trusted the guy."

"Are we done assessing blame?" Gavin asked. "Can we move on to how the hell we're going to get out of this?"

"Are you really all right?"

"I'll survive. Okay, let's start at the beginning. Tell me everything that happened."

There wasn't much to tell, as it turned out. Fake cop, a lie about a parking-lot wreck, some chloroform, and *bam!* It was done. Her attacker had been a stranger, but clearly he'd targeted her.

"I think the cell phone is broken," she said. "I'm not even sure where it is, and I can't see a damn thing in here. But maybe since you can use both your hands, you can figure out what's wrong with it."

"Wait a minute. What's wrong with your hands?"

"I'm tied up."

"Oh for— Why didn't you tell me that?" He crawled toward the sound of her voice until he felt her warmth. Then he reached out to touch her. He connected with her shoulder. She was shaking. "Give me your hands."

She swiveled around. Her hands were tied behind her with some sort of soft scarf. Gavin immediately saw the implications, and they didn't please him.

The knot was easy to undo just by feel. He had her free in a few seconds. He tucked the scarf into his pocket. Might be useful at some point.

"Oh, thank you," she said. "That feels much better."

"Are your feet tied, too?"

"Not for long."

"Is there anything in the truck that can be used for a weapon?" Gavin asked, getting back to the practical. He felt around the floor of the truck until his hand settled on something small and hard. "I think I found your cell phone. Or most of it, anyway."

"The truck was empty when he tossed me in here,"

she said. "It's just us, my purse and four-dozen Krispy Kreme doughnuts. Oh, and a bottle of glass cleaner."

"That has possibilities. What's in your purse?"

She handed the butter-soft suede bag to him. "My wallet. Some makeup—lip gloss, powder, a mascara, I think. A packet of tissues. Oh, there might be a nail file. A calculator. Moist towelettes."

He tried the cell phone first. But he could feel that the case was cracked, and he couldn't get it to come on. He found the nail file, a flimsy thing with a dull point. Still, it had potential. He tucked that into his pocket next to the scarf.

"Oh, my God," she said suddenly.

"What?"

"There's a little Swiss Army knife in an inner zipper compartment. My dad gave it to me years ago. I hardly ever use it."

Gavin searched around until he found the tiny knife. It wasn't much, but it was sharp. He handed it to Shelby. "Keep this somewhere handy. We don't know how much time we have. But the truck's been moving steadily for a while, now. We must be on the highway."

"Where do you suppose he's taking us?"

"Somewhere isolated, is my guess. Shelby, I need to tell you some things I've figured out. They're not very cheerful. But you need to know, so we can be as prepared as possible."

"Okay. Oh, my God, do you think this guy is some kind of sadistic serial killer? Is that it? Is he going to torture us to death?"

"I don't think so. A serial killer generally works alone. This guy has a partner—I saw him in the truck.

And a serial killer generally targets victims of opportunity. You've hardly been an easy victim. Three different kidnapping attempts. Three different perpetrators. The first two are dead—one of them murdered, probably because he knew what was going on."

"So one person is behind all the kidnappings. He hired these thugs to grab me. And when Paulie Sapp failed, he killed him to keep him from talking."

"Exactly. Think, Shelby. Someone out there really has it in for you. You don't have any enemies? A stalker? A thwarted boyfriend? A rival at work? A family member who stands to inherit a fortune if you die first?"

"I'm thinking. But no one comes to mind. No creepy co-workers or would-be boyfriends. No greedy family members. I'm an only child. My grandparents left me a trust. When I die Jake gets it—but my parents are named as trustees. And they have plenty of their own money, believe me." She took a shaky breath. "Oh, Jake. I don't want him to grow up without a mother."

Gavin longed to comfort Shelby, but they had to be practical. "Don't think about that now."

"Paulie Sapp said something about trying to get a ransom for me."

"I thought of that, too. But a couple of things lead me to believe you were never intended to get out of this alive. The first thing is that all three kidnappers have let you see their faces. They know you can identify them. The second thing…" He debated about whether to tell her.

"Go ahead."

"Most kidnappers use duct tape or zip ties to bind their victims. Or nylon cord. Or even a piece of nylon stocking. But this guy used a thick, soft scarf at your wrists. And a cattle prod, which won't do permanent damage."

"Because he didn't want to hurt me."

"Because he doesn't want to leave any type of mark that would indicate foul play."

"When they find my body," she said dully.

"He also chose to asphyxiate you, rather than hitting you over the head or injecting a drug. My guess is he wanted to use something that wouldn't show up…" He couldn't say the rest.

"…in an autopsy," Shelby finished for him. "So he's going to stage an accident."

"That's my theory, anyway."

"But where? Timbuktu? Where are we going?"

"Is there any place out of town you routinely visit?" Gavin asked.

"My parents. They live in Austin while the legislature's in session. They have a house on Lake Travis."

"That could be it. An accidental drowning would work."

"But the truck wasn't headed in the right direction to reach Austin."

"He might be going in a roundabout way, trying to avoid witnesses."

"This is depressing," Shelby said.

"I'm sorry. But the more we can figure out about this guy's intentions, his mind-set, the easier it will be to trip him up."

"Do you think there's a chance?"

"There's always a chance. This guy didn't count on me showing up. Right now, he's wondering how he's going to neutralize me. Include me in your accident?

Who would believe you'd taken me to visit your parents? Maybe fix it so it looks like *I* kidnapped and killed you, then killed myself? That has possibilities. If I were him, that's what I'd do."

"One of my parolees tried to kill his wife by faking a car wreck," Shelby said. "He didn't succeed, thank God. One thing I learned going over his file—it's really hard to fake something like that. The forensics experts analyze every drop of blood spatter, the skid marks—everything—to recreate the accident. If things don't add up, they start looking for suspects."

"If they have suspicions in the first place. And if they don't assign lazy Lyle to the case. At any rate," Gavin continued, "this guy is going to be panicking a little bit. Maybe he's talking it over with whoever hired him. There's a second person in the truck with him."

"Could it be Owen?" Shelby asked in a small voice. "What did he look like?"

"I was a little busy and didn't get a good look. Whoever it is, he didn't lift a finger when the fake cop and I were fighting. Can Owen fight?"

"Yeah, he can throw a punch," Shelby said bitterly. "I just can't think of anyone else who might want me dead, even though I still think he doesn't have a motive. He doesn't hate me."

"But you're the one who filed for divorce?"

"Yes."

"Why? Oh, hell, never mind. You don't have to talk about this. I was just going into cop mode, asking rude questions and expecting to get answers."

She answered anyway. "He'd always been kind of…dramatic. I liked that at first. You know, like he'd die if he couldn't have me and he loved me so much he couldn't think about anything else. But once we were married, he didn't mellow out the way I thought he would. He became very possessive, very jealous, though there was no reason for him to be. He even questioned whether Jake was really his."

"Was he ever violent?"

"No. Well, he never hit me. He yelled sometimes. Slammed doors. Broke a glass one time, threw it at a brick wall. I guess I was crazy to think having a baby would help. I left him pretty soon after Jake was born."

"How'd he react?"

"Wanted me back. Said he'd change. But he'd made those promises before. When he saw I was serious, he accepted it and turned his attention to getting as much out of the settlement as he could."

"He sounds like a classic abuser."

"I went to a therapist for a while during the divorce. She said the same thing. She said he would have escalated if I hadn't gotten out."

"Abusers very often kill their wives, or ex-wives. Have you done anything to set him off recently? Like, have you started seeing someone?" He held his breath, far more interested in her answer than he should have been.

"No. I haven't even gone out on a date since the divorce. I thought I could happily live the rest of my life single and celibate. That was before I met you."

Suddenly the air around them seemed to be charged with electricity. Though it was pitch-dark in the truck, Gavin could have sworn he saw blue sparks arcing between them.

He'd never expected her to say anything like that. In

fact, he'd assumed she would ignore and forget the kiss they'd shared.

"Did I shock you?" she asked.

"Mildly."

"Well, if I'm going to die, no reason to leave things unsaid." Her tone was practical. "I was attracted to you from the moment we met. I like to think I did a pretty good job of staying professional, though, until recently."

"Professional? More like an ice princess."

"You thawed me out." She laughed nervously. Then she reached toward him, fumbling until she found his hand and squeezed it. "Sorry. I'm probably embarrassing you. But all this talk of murder and dying makes me think. Do I want the last few minutes or hours of my life to be spent alone, terrified, or do I want to reach out to someone I've grown fond of, someone I like and trust and respect? What have I got to lose, after all?"

He pulled her to him and held her. The embrace was awkward—there was nothing to support them, no soft pillows. He scooted around until he could sit back against the wall of the truck, then let her lean against him.

They were quiet for a few minutes, simply letting the silent connection hum between them. He could have stayed like that forever, just holding Shelby as he had many times in his dreams, sitting in the dark, the hum of the truck's engine lulling them into a false sense of security. As long as that engine kept running, as long as the truck kept moving, nothing could happen to them.

After a while, though, Gavin forced himself to again be practical. "Did you say there were doughnuts in here?"

"Yeah. Krispy Kreme. One of the boxes got squashed, but the others are around here somewhere."

Releasing him reluctantly, she felt around until she found one of the cardboard boxes and opened it. "I think these are the plain glazed ones."

"My favorite. Dig in. Eat as many as you can. We'll need our strength for whatever's coming."

SHELBY FORCED HERSELF to eat four doughnuts, though they tasted like cardboard to her and sat like lumps of lead in her stomach. "How many did you eat?" she asked.

"I'm on my sixth. You want to make something of it?"

"If you can eat six doughnuts and not feel sick, then your head injury must not be too serious."

"You're right. I'll take my good news where I can get it."

"So now that we're fortified with plenty of fat and sugar, what's next?"

"We need a plan. When the truck stops, we make as much noise as possible—beating on the sides of the truck, shouting, stomping. Maybe someone will hear us."

"But probably not. He won't stop anywhere with people around."

"What if he needs gas?"

"If he can't find an isolated gas pump, he'll park somewhere and walk to the station. He probably has a container."

"Now you're thinking like a criminal," Gavin said, encouraging her. "Assuming no one comes to our rescue, sooner or later our man will have to open the back door. When he does, we'll be ready."

"If we wait right by the door, he'll just get us with the cattle prod. And trust me, once he does that, we won't be capable of much else. That thing hurts."

"But he can't get us both at once. He'll go for me first—I'm his biggest threat. While he's going for me, you get him in the face with the window cleaner. I'll try to get the cattle prod away from him, or stab him with the nail file."

She groaned. "This is not a very good plan. What about his partner, the guy in the passenger seat?" She refused to think of that person as Owen. It just couldn't be Owen. She couldn't have married a murderer.

"That guy'll be easy," Gavin said with exaggerated confidence, to prop her up, no doubt. "He's such a wuss, he wouldn't even help his friend while I was beating the crap out of him. We can do this, Shelby. At the very worst, we can force them to deviate from their plan."

"You mean we can force them to kill us in a way they weren't planning on."

"Well, yeah. I wasn't going to say it that way. But as long as we're on the subject, we should leave as much biological evidence as we can in this truck. Blood, saliva, hair."

Shelby whimpered. She couldn't help it. She preferred her blood to stay in her body where it belonged.

"Look," he said gently, "I want to live. I want us both to live real bad. I mean, you just said all those nice things to me about liking me and trusting me and respecting me, and you said you were attracted to me. If those aren't strong motivation to survive, I don't know what is. But if things go bad, if we don't make it, well, I just want those sons of bitches to get caught."

Chapter Eight

Shelby pulled herself together. If she had to die, she wasn't going to do it whimpering and cringing like a beaten dog. She would go down fighting. What Gavin was saying made sense. If, after the two of them met their end, this truck came up suspicious, crime-scene technicians would go over every inch of it. Blood could be washed away, but small remnants always remained in crevices. DNA testing was so sophisticated these days, the crime lab only needed a few molecules for proof.

"I can cut myself with the pocket knife."

"Sterilize it with the window cleaner first."

"If I live long enough to worry about an infection, I'll be a happy camper." Still, she did as he suggested, spraying window cleaner on the small knife blade.

"The blade is sharp. Don't overdo it."

"I'll cut my arm," she said. "I don't want to risk injuring a fingertip. I'll need my hands."

"Good thinking."

She pushed up the sleeve of her sweater, took a deep breath and made a shallow cut about an inch long, then checked to make sure she'd actually produced blood.

She felt something dripping off her arm. Damn, she hoped she didn't bleed to death.

"Well, that wasn't so bad." She wiped the knife off on her jeans and folded it closed, then handed it to Gavin. "Maybe you better keep this. I wouldn't know how to use it as a weapon. You don't have to stick yourself, though. You already bled enough, from your head wound. In fact, I'm more worried about whether you've *stopped* bleeding." She allowed blood to drip from her arm onto the floor of the truck, then smeared it around, making sure she got some into the crack between floor and wall. As she did so, she noticed a feature in the truck she hadn't paid much attention to before.

"Hey, Gavin, I have an idea. Let's leave bite marks on these rubber cushioning strips. They can't just wash those away. They would have to replace them."

"You're really getting into this."

"It feels good to be taking some sort of action, even if it's kind of morbid to be thinking about things that will help after we're dead."

"Like I said, this is our backup plan. I'm counting on us getting out of this alive."

Shelby washed a section of the rubber strip with window cleaner, then bit into it several times, making sure she left impressions of both upper and lower teeth. "Blech, this rubber tastes awful. God knows what sort of germs we're picking up. My mother would have a fit if she knew what I was doing."

"I imagine mine would, too," Gavin said softly, and she could tell he was thinking about his family. He'd told her how supportive they were, how much they'd wanted to help him when he'd been released from prison. At first he'd refused to see them. He hadn't wanted them to see how far he'd fallen, and he was worried about how they would receive him, though they'd spoken on his behalf at his parole hearing. But Shelby had convinced him that getting his family's emotional support was key to ensuring his success on the outside.

He'd made an appearance at his sister's wedding to Beau Maddox, reporting afterward that his family had welcomed him back like the prodigal son he was. And Beau, who had once been like a brother to him, had wanted only to repair their friendship and move forward.

"Tell me more about your family," she said once they'd left as many clues in the truck as they could think of.

"I'd like it better if you'd tell me about yours," he said. "The whole time you were my parole officer, you asked questions and I answered them. I think it's time we turned the tables."

"Okay." She took a deep breath. Opening herself up had always been difficult for her. She'd been raised to be very private. With a father in politics, she couldn't be airing dirty linen to anyone.

Not that there was much. "You already figured out my family has money. My father is a bigwig in state politics. I was raised in Payton, went to St. Anne's Preparatory."

"You Catholic schoolgirls have a reputation for being wild, you know. It's all that repression."

"Well, I'm Presbyterian. I wasn't repressed. And I wasn't wild."

"Those high-heel shoes you wear say otherwise."

So he'd noticed her little fetish. "I like shoes. I have

to stick to a shoe budget, or my mortgage money would go to Prada."

"That's kind of kinky."

"Oh, stop it. Everyone has some little peculiarity like that. I bet you have one."

"Yeah. I have a thing for good girls with a wild streak." He crawled toward her in the darkness, then pulled her against him, again encouraging her to pillow her head against his shoulder. "The first time I saw you, all I could think about was pulling the pins out of your hair and smearing your perfect lipstick. You were so…cool. So remote. Such an ice princess.

"And that turned you on, huh?"

"Big-time. I kept wondering why such a refined lady chose such an oddball job. I mean, with your background, you could have done anything. You could be a lawyer, a doctor, a CEO. Or you could have married one of the above and become a country-club wife who dabbles in a favorite charity."

"Please. I don't think it's right to use family money or connections to get what you want out of life. I don't even like to tell people who my father is. I make my own way."

"Why a parole officer?"

"You really want to know?"

"Of course."

"My best friend in junior high was Kathy Aikin. Her father was an accountant for a big oil company. I forget which one. But he got caught with his hand in the cookie jar, and he went away for a while.

"Well, it was just devastating for the family, as you can imagine. They had to sell their nice house, their cars, their boat, jewelry, everything. Kathy dropped out of St. Anne's and went to public school.

"But they were coping. Until her dad was paroled. Then it was just so horrible. He couldn't get a job washing windows, much less anything in his field. He just sat around the house all day eating potato chips and watching soap operas. It tore the family apart. Clearly the system had forgotten him. And then one day Kathy came home from school to find him hanging from the kitchen light fixture."

"Oh, God."

"She was never the same after that. She dropped out, ran off with some lowlife.

"The whole thing made a huge impression on me. I wanted to help. I wanted to fix the parole system and make sure that never happened to another family. Of course, I soon realized I couldn't fix the whole system. But I thought I could fix my own little corner of it. So that's what I try to do.

"I'm not always successful." A vision of Manny Cruz floated into her brain. She squelched it immediately. She couldn't afford to get maudlin now.

"You succeeded with me."

"You were going to succeed no matter who was supervising you."

"Maybe. But I worked extra hard to earn your approval. Every word of praise you gave me, I hung on to. You're making a difference. Trust me."

She snuggled up closer to him. "Thank you."

THEY RODE FOR HOURS. The truck stopped twice. Each time, Shelby and Gavin beat on the sides of the truck and screamed for help at the tops of their lungs. But they got no results. Gavin figured the driver had stopped at big, noisy truck stops where he could pull up to a remote pump. Gavin could hear diesel engines passing by during the brief periods they were stopped.

"Where could they possibly be taking us?" Shelby asked for the tenth time.

Gavin finally answered her. "As far away from Payton as possible. It will take longer to match up our bodies with the missing-persons report."

"Oh, that's cheerful."

"You asked. I'm guessing we're headed for some massive wilderness area, where our bodies might never be discovered. Maybe this is Plan B, since my appearance mucked up Plan A, whatever that was."

The truck rumbled on. They made an effort not to be maudlin about dying or never seeing their loved ones again. Instead, they talked about everything, from books to music to cars, and Gavin was surprised at the things they had in common. They'd both hated geometry class and loved calculus—what were the chances of that? They both took guilty pleasure in watching old sitcoms, everything from *I Love Lucy* to *Gilligan's Island*.

"So who would you rather be stranded with," Shelby asked, "Ginger or Mary Ann?"

"No contest. Mary Ann, in a heartbeat. Those little short shorts she wore, and the crop tops—way sexier than Ginger's over-the-top evening gowns."

"Right. The good-girl thing. What about Samantha Stevens and Jeannie? Which one would you rather go to bed with?"

"Guess."

"I think you're a Samantha fan."

"Those nose twitches drove me nuts. Jeannie was way too obvious and pushy, not to mention a little dense. What about you? Fonzie or Richie Cunningham?"

"No contest. The Fonz."

"So you like bad boys."

"I *married* a bad boy. I discovered they're much better in fantasies than in real life."

"Hmm. Doesn't say much for my chances."

She didn't have a reply to that, and he knew he'd made her uncomfortable. She'd opened up to him because she thought they were going to die—not because she had some deep-seated need to bond with him. He needed to remember that. If they somehow managed to get out of this alive, she would be embarrassed as hell at all the things they'd talked about.

They ate some more doughnuts, though the cloying sweetness was getting on Gavin's nerves. "I used to crave these things when I was in prison. Worse than I even craved drugs, sometimes."

"If we get out of this alive, I'll never eat another one. They're just making me thirstier."

"Let's not talk about that." Their lack of water had Gavin worried. They were already dehydrated. If they didn't get something to drink soon, they would really start to suffer. "It's getting colder. Did you notice?"

"Yeah, now that you mention it. Think we're heading north?"

"Maybe. But I also think we could be headed into some mountains. The truck has slowed down, and it's making a lot of turns."

"That would fit with your wilderness theory."

As another hour dragged by, the temperature drop was more noticeable, as was the truck's slower pace and the twisty path. Definitely mountains. Sometimes the truck would lurch or skid, indicating they were traveling through snow or ice.

He could feel Shelby shivering, even nestled in the crook of his arm. "You want my sweatshirt? I'm not that cold," he lied.

"I'm not that cold, either," she fibbed back.

Abruptly the truck's engine died. Shelby tensed. Gabe strained his ears to listen.

"Another gas stop?"

"Too soon for that."

"Maybe we got stopped by a cop."

"Dream on." The driver's door opened and closed. The lock at the back of the truck rattled. "C'mon, this is it. Just like we talked about it."

Shelby scrambled for the window cleaner. Gavin opened the pocket knife. The tiny blade wasn't much, but if he could strike to the face or throat, it would do its job.

He'd never killed anyone before, not even close. Still, he believed he could do it to save his life. To save Shelby's life.

They crouched at opposite ends of the door, which would force their kidnapper to choose one or the other. Whoever was left could attack.

The door opened suddenly, but the man on the other side jumped out of the way. Gavin lunged for him and missed—and hell, it was dark as pitch outside. Trapped in the dark truck, he'd lost all sense of time.

Gavin landed on snow-covered ground just as their adversary shouted, "Freeze, both of you. I've got a gun."

Oh, hell. Gavin had expected their friend to have a gun. Still, it added a whole new dimension to their situation. He froze where he stood. Even if he'd wanted to ignore the warning, he couldn't see his target. He quickly pocketed the knife.

The other man switched on a flashlight and shined it in Gavin's face. Gavin held out his hands in a gesture of surrender.

"Well, I see you survived. That's good."

"It is?" Gavin asked. He was looking for Shelby wondering where she was. But the flashlight in his face blinded him.

"I'm not out to murder anyone. This is a kidnap for ransom. You two cooperate, you'll be released unharmed in a day or two. Shelby, out of the truck. I see you managed to get yourself untied. Now put down the glass cleaner, for chrissakes. Did you really think you were going to hurt me with that?"

"I thought so, yeah," Shelby said defiantly. Gavin heard her jump out of the truck and into the snow.

"Both of you turn around and put your hands on the truck where I can see them. And don't even think about making a run for it. You might get away. But in this cold, you'd die of exposure in a matter of hours. We are way, way far away from any other humans."

Gavin did as requested. The kidnapper was no longer shining the flashlight directly in Gavin's eyes, so he could see some. The guy did, indeed, have a gun—looked like a .38, which was no pea shooter—and he had it pointed directly at Shelby. If Gavin attempted any heroics at this point, he could get Shelby killed. The guy was also wearing a down parka. So this was not Plan B after all. He'd known he would be coming to the mountains where it would be cold.

And it definitely was cold. A chill wind whistled through towering pine trees. Gavin could see the trees, now that the moon had come out from behind the clouds. The truck was parked in a clearing.

The man approached Gavin first. "Don't look at me," he said gruffly. "I've got the gun trained on your girlfriend here, Sir Galahad. You so much as twitch, she gets it between the eyes. I don't want to kill either of you. That doesn't mean I won't. I'm not going back to prison."

Gavin understood that motivation clearly enough. At one time he'd have done just about anything to stay on the outside—including point a gun at his former best friend and colleague. He understood desperation. And he had a healthy respect for it. He could not count on the guy's threat to be a bluff.

Gavin heard the *rip-rip-rip* of duct tape.

"Feet together," the man said.

Gavin complied, though as his feet were being wrapped, he separated his ankles as much as he thought he could get away with without being too obvious, to give himself some wiggle room. He also covertly peered at the kidnapper. The flashlight glittered off a brass name tag on his fake cop uniform—P. Rodney. Undoubtedly not his real name, but that was what Gavin decided to call him.

Rodney bound Gavin's wrists behind his back.

The moon peeked out again, and Gavin caught a glimpse of Shelby out of the corner of his eye. She was leaning against the truck bed, her hair disheveled and falling across her face. She shivered so hard he could see it.

Rodney told Gavin to sit and keep his eyes on the ground. Then he went to work on Shelby, again binding her wrists with a scarf, still keeping with his plan. He deftly managed the task one-handed with the use of his teeth. With his other hand, he kept the gun pointed directly at Gavin.

Gavin considered, then rejected a number of moves. He would only get himself killed. And he was far more disposable than Shelby. Nobody was going to pay a huge ransom for his safe return. He doubted Rodney would hesitate long and hard before shooting Gavin dead.

Shelby sniffed a couple of times. He hoped she wasn't crying. He didn't think he could take it if she started crying.

Rodney didn't gag them. That probably meant there was no one within a hundred miles who would hear them calling for help.

In one deft move, Rodney hefted Shelby over his shoulder. "You," he said to Gavin, gesturing with the gun. "Don't move a muscle 'til I get back."

Gavin didn't honor the order with a response. What was he supposed to do, hop down the mountain? Roll? If only he had use of his feet, he *would* run. If he had something sharp to cut that duct tape with…

The truck engine clunked, making a settling-down noise. Engines were hot. Duct tape might melt. The exhaust pipe—that was it. Gavin maneuvered himself close to the truck's exhaust pipe—thank God it was an old truck that didn't conceal the pipe for safety reasons. He then pressed his bound ankles directly against the still-hot pipe.

The tape melted like butter, sizzling and producing a nauseating smell of burning plastic—and burning flesh. He stifled a cry of pain. Damn, he was in too much of a hurry. But the burn on his ankles was worth it when he felt the tape weakening. With a few yanks, Gavin pulled his legs free of the bindings.

He didn't waste any time. He took off into the woods, praying Rodney's partner couldn't see him. Without benefit of flashlight or a bright moon, he was navigating blind. Branches slapped him in the face. He tripped over falling logs, and twice smacked into tree trunks.

"Hey!" he heard Rodney calling. "What do you think you're doing?"

Gavin hid behind a tree. If Rodney came after him, perhaps he could ambush him, take the gun away…all with his hands tied behind his back? He wished he'd paid more attention when Lori talked about kicking. Still, he had to do something. If he got himself killed, Shelby didn't stand a chance.

He could hear Rodney crashing through the woods, drawing closer. His flashlight bobbed up and down as he followed Gavin's path. Tracking Gavin through the snow would be child's play.

"I will shoot you like the dog you are," Rodney yelled. "It's no skin off my nose. Shelby's the one with the rich daddy."

Gavin waited, scarcely breathing. It was bitterly cold, and the snow was coming down harder now. And Rodney had almost reached Gavin's hiding place.

"I know right where you are," Rodney said, circling wide, trying to get a better vantage point. Then he switched off the flashlight, and Gavin couldn't see him.

Several tense seconds passed. Then, the crack of the gun discharging, and a bullet whizzing past Gavin's head.

The flashlight switched back on. "Did I hit you, you loser?"

He hadn't missed by much. The futility of Gavin's situation was almost overwhelming. Then, he got an idea. He dropped to the ground. "I'm hit! I'm hurt bad." He injected as much anguish into his cries as he could. "Oh, God, help me. Please help me, I'm dying."

"Too bad, dude," Rodney said softly. "They probably won't even pay me extra for this." His footsteps receded into the night.

SHELBY LAY ON HER BACK on a small iron bed with a bare mattress, in a rustic mountain cabin. The kidnapper had untied her hands long enough for her to choke down a tuna-fish sandwich and a bottle of water, which had tasted like nectar of the gods. But he'd quickly trussed her up again, this time with her hands above her head, tied to the foot of the iron bed. Her feet were still taped together.

She tried not to think about the gunshot she'd heard a few minutes earlier—or the fact that Gavin had not been brought inside the cabin. The kidnapper had refused to answer any questions.

He'd built a fire so she wouldn't freeze overnight. Then he'd left, announcing he would see her in the morning. She deemed it a good sign that the man had given her food and water. He obviously had some motivation for keeping her alive. But Gavin—she couldn't think about that now.

She was too scared to sleep. She'd tried to escape

from her bindings, but the scarf around her wrists was too tight. And she'd never realized duct tape, wrapped around her ankles, could be so strong. The stuff could probably be used to fasten the wings onto airplanes.

She tried maneuvering to get her feet on the floor, but that didn't work. Then she got a brainstorm. She could roll backward and do a somersault over the foot of the bed.

Once again calling on her yoga training, she went into a shoulder stand, then slowly lowered her legs over her head. Her silk bindings were only wrapped once around the top rail of the bedstead, so they swiveled with her body as she lowered her legs toward the floor.

She could only maintain the balance for so long; the last couple of feet she fell, banging her head on the hard iron bed. But her feet were on the floor, her wrists weren't broken. If she could find something sharp, maybe she could rub the scarf up against it and saw her way free.

As she pondered the problem, she heard a noise at the door. Oh, Lord, not now. Why had he come back so soon?

The door opened. "Shelby?"

"Gavin!" Her heart leaped with joy. "You're not dead!"

"Close, but not this time. Are you alone?" He stepped inside, cautiously looking around. The fire had died down to embers, and the cabin was mostly in shadow.

"The kidnapper is gone. I'm almost free but I wouldn't mind a little help."

"Where's the light?"

She could hear him feeling around for a light switch. "There's an old lantern by the fireplace."

She heard his footsteps moving across the plank floor

toward the fireplace. Gavin fumbled around, then a match flared to life and he lit the old kerosene lamp. He moved closer to her, holding up the lamp so he could examine her.

"Are you all right?"

"I'm fine. Just, please, get me untied. What happened? How'd you get free? I heard a gunshot—I was sure you were dead."

"First chance I got, I ran out into the woods. I fooled Rodney into thinking he'd killed me. I don't think he's the brightest bulb in the lamp shop."

"Rodney?"

"That's what his name tag says. I'm sure it's not his real name, but I'm calling him that for convenience's sake."

As he set the lantern down, she got her first good look at him since the ordeal had begun, and she almost wished she hadn't. "Oh, Gavin, you're hurt." Half his face was covered with dried blood, and his sweater sported a large, red-brown stain.

"I'm okay. I've still got your Swiss Army knife. I'll have you free in no time."

He did. And the moment Shelby had full use of her arms and legs, she used them to launch herself into Gavin's embrace. Gavin's mouth found hers in the flickering lantern light, and they were kissing.

Chapter Nine

Gavin had never felt anything as wonderful as Shelby's mouth against his, so warm and soft and female. Her body was so full of life.

Yes, they were still alive! And for the first time, he truly believed they could remain that way. They had until daylight to formulate a plan.

Shelby broke the kiss and stared at him, her eyes filled with worry. "I can't stand seeing you like this." She found her purse, which Rodney had brought inside, and dug around until she located a moist towelette. Gavin patiently allowed her to clean the blood from his face and examine his injuries.

"Well, I can't see much in this light. But I think you've stopped bleeding, at least. And the burn on your leg doesn't look too serious. Let's get out of here before Rodney gets back. We need to find you a doctor."

"We can't just run," he said sensibly. "It's cold out there, and snowing. We'd die of exposure in a matter of hours."

"But we could follow the road, flag down a motorist…."

"There might not be any motorists. If the passes are closed because of weather, or if we're just too remote, we could freeze to death waiting to be rescued."

"But we can't just sit here waiting for Rodney like a couple of sitting ducks." Her voice took on a slight edge of hysteria. "Not after we've worked so hard to get loose."

He rubbed her shoulders. "We won't be sitting ducks, not by a long shot. We'll arm ourselves. Let's search every inch of this cabin for something we can use as a weapon. I wish I knew where the hell we are."

"I know," Shelby said dully. "I've been here before."

Gavin was relieved. "Where are we?"

"Peavy, Colorado. And you're right, it is way up in the Rockies and miles from any town or even a decent road. I only spent one miserable weekend here although it felt like a month. I remember it way too well. This is Owen's fishing cabin."

Gavin cursed. "Hell, I'm sorry, Shelby."

"Guess that just about cinches it. The father of my child wants me dead. Oh, God, that means Jake's in danger, too!"

Gavin pulled her to him again, but not for a passionate embrace this time. He simply held her, knowing he probably brought her little comfort. He couldn't imagine what it felt like to know that someone you'd once loved and trusted, someone with whom you'd brought a child into the world, was a murderer.

"Maybe he only wants money. You said his finances are shaky."

"Owen is always in financial straits. He has a real knack for living beyond his means. He kept thinking he'd land a really big case and pay off his debts. But he's not a particularly good lawyer, and so far his big case hasn't come along."

"So he might have a real motive for trying to get a ransom. Particularly if, like you said, he can't get his hands on yours or Jake's money no matter what."

Shelby brightened. "He can't, and he knows it. Maybe he really isn't trying to kill me."

"It doesn't mean we won't end up dead. This guy he hired to do his dirty work, this Rodney—he doesn't seem like a guy with a lot of compunction. And there've been plenty of kidnappers who have collected ransom for a dead victim."

"You're always so cheery."

"I just don't want you to get complacent. We're still fighting for our lives. For sure, there's not much reason to keep me alive. I mean, he did shoot at me once already."

"I thought I heard shots earlier, but then I thought it must have been a branch cracking from the weight of the snow. My God, what happened?"

He gave her the condensed version of his aborted escape attempt.

"Oh, Gavin, it's just as well you didn't get away. You'd have died out there, no coat, no good shoes. Now we have a fighting chance."

They explored the tiny, rustic cabin with the lantern. It was just the one room, with a bare plank floor and vaulted ceiling supported by two rough-pine pillars. The room was furnished simply with a bed, a rickety table, a couple of basic wooden chairs and one ancient armchair with its stuffing coming out. It had only two small windows, and no light was visible through them.

A few primitive cooking utensils sat on the stone hearth next to the fireplace.

But there was a pile of boxes stacked in one corner that interested Gavin. He brought the lantern close so he could investigate. The boxes appeared crisp and clean, with labels like Land's End and Eddie Bauer.

"If this is what I think it is, we're in luck." He used the rusty kitchen knife to slit open all the boxes, then started removing the contents, increasingly optimistic with each treasure he uncovered. One box held a backpack. Another had a sleeping bag. There was a good quality jacket, gloves, hiking boots, thermal underwear. Gavin even found a whole bag of Clif Bars, a backpacker's staple, and a twelve-pack of bottled water.

"This is great!" Shelby tried on the jacket. "It fits me. Is there another one that might fit you?" She rummaged through the boxes and packing material. Foam peanuts flew in every direction. But there was only one set of everything, and all of it fit Shelby, even the boots.

The conclusion was inescapable. This stuff had all been purchased for Shelby. Gavin grabbed a packing slip and examined it. "This was bought with your credit card."

"No way." Shelby examined the piece of yellow paper. "Oh, my God, you're right. Owen must have stolen my credit card. Where's my purse?"

The suede bag had been thrown into a corner. Shelby took out her wallet and checked the contents. "All my cards are still here."

"He probably just copied down the number, then ordered by phone. He bought all the camping gear with your card so it would appear that you'd planned a vacation getaway. He'll probably tell the police you asked if you could borrow the cabin."

"Then there's no ransom," Shelby concluded dully. "That was just a fairy tale to get us to cooperate."

"That's my guess. But it doesn't matter what he planned. He won't get away with it. He's left a paper trail all over the place. I mean, he had to have this stuff shipped somewhere." The shipping labels had been torn off, he noticed. "Land's End and Eddie Bauer will have a record of it. He's toast."

Shelby pulled off the knit cap she'd tried on and scratched her head. "You know, Owen's a slime bucket, but he's not stupid. How could he make a careless mistake like that?"

Gavin shrugged. "Criminals always make mistakes, even the brilliant ones. There is no perfect crime."

"Okay, here's my plan. I'll put all this stuff on, walk down the mountain and get help."

"How far is it to the nearest town?"

"Um…twenty miles?"

Gavin shook his head. "No way."

"I can do it. I'm in good shape."

"You can't walk twenty miles through two or three feet of snow in blizzard conditions. Have you looked out the window?"

"It's too dark to see anything."

"Exactly. You'll either fall into a snowdrift and be buried, or you'll walk off the side of a mountain."

"I'll wait until it's light."

"Rodney will be back when it's light."

"Well, what's your plan, Einstein?" She sounded a bit put out.

"We set a trap. There's only one door, and Rodney has to come through it. Something very bad will happen when he does."

"What?"

"I haven't figured that part out yet. But while I'm thinking, why don't you put on that thermal underwear? You're shivering again."

Shelby looked around. "There's nowhere to get undressed."

He gave her a look. "Pick any dark corner. Hell, I'll turn around. Now is not the time to be modest."

She gave him a tight nod and retreated to somewhere beyond the lantern's reach. He turned his back as if he were a gentleman and listened to the rustle of clothes sliding over skin. He tried not to get too turned on thinking about Shelby minus her clothes. As he'd just said, this was not the time. His body didn't cooperate, though.

WHEN A GRAY DAWN began peeking through the windows, Gavin was satisfied with the plan they'd devised. It was ninety-nine percent perfect. But that one percent still had him worried. There was always something that could go wrong.

While they waited for Rodney to return, they gave the cabin a more thorough search with the help of daylight through the windows. To Gavin's relief, they found a footlocker lodged under the iron bed that contained clothing—an old down jacket, gloves, wool socks and a pair of cracked leather boots. They were Owen's, and looked close to the right size for Gavin. He was freezing, but they couldn't restart the fire because smoke coming from the chimney might alarm Rodney. Gavin donned the warm clothes.

They each ate a Clif bar and drank some of the bottled water.

As gray dawn gave way to a clear, bright morning, they heard the truck engine approaching. Gavin peered out the tiny window that served as a peephole in the door. The truck soon pulled into the clearing.

The sun reflected brightly off the truck's windshield, so Gavin couldn't see who all was inside. But only one person got out—Rodney, who'd been driving. He probably had his gun on him somewhere, but it wasn't in his hand as he approached the cabin. So far, so good.

"Get in position," he told Shelby. "You're sure you can do this?"

"I won't even hesitate," she said, though whether it was to convince him or herself, he didn't know. She shrank against the wall next to the door, where Rodney wouldn't be able to see her. In her hands she held a huge cast-iron skillet.

Gavin took his position, crouching behind the bed. His job was to leap on Rodney after Shelby had stunned him, and subdue him. He could only hope that at first glance, Rodney would think all was as he left it. They wanted him to be all the way inside the cabin before Shelby whacked him. They had to prevent Rodney's silent partner from witnessing the attack, so he would think everything was okay.

The door latch rattled, then the door opened and Rodney stepped inside. His gaze went immediately to the bed. The empty bed.

"Hey—" That was the last word Rodney said for

a while. With a stunned expression, he went down on his knees, then crumpled to the floor.

"Oh, my God, did I kill him?" Shelby asked in a scared voice, dropping the frying pan with a loud clatter.

Gavin pounced on the man, quickly locating the .38 revolver and holding it out to Shelby, butt first. "Take this."

"What? No. I hate guns."

"And I'm not supposed to touch guns, remember?"

"Gavin, I'm not going to—"

"I'm not going back to prison."

"Oh, for the love of—fine, give it to me. I'll put it in my purse. Did I kill the guy or not?"

Rodney groaned.

"Apparently not." Gavin quickly bound Rodney's hands behind him, using the scarf that had been used on Shelby. Then he tied Rodney's feet with some clothesline he'd found earlier. "Look out the peephole," he said to Shelby. "Tell me what's going on out there."

Shelby did as Gavin asked. Then she cursed like a sailor. It was the first time Gavin had ever heard her use language like that. He jumped to his feet, ready for action.

"What?" he demanded. "Is something happening?"

"The truck! It's leaving!"

"Hell. That was our only means to get off this mountain. Rodney's partner in crime must have realized something was wrong and got the hell out of Dodge." Gavin nudged Rodney's leg with his foot. "Nice company you keep. Real loyal. When the chips are down, he turned tail and ran."

"Why do you call me Rodney?"

"Your phony police name tag." The police uniform

was gone, now, replaced by a ski bib and flannel shirt. "What *should* I call you?"

The man was stubbornly silent. He obviously wasn't going to volunteer any information.

"I'm sorry I hit you so hard," Shelby said. "Does it hurt?"

"Shelby!" Gavin barked. "This is the guy who drugged you and hit me in the head with a bumper. He tried to kill me, twice, and if given half a chance he'll try again. Make sure that gun stays out of his reach."

"I will. But two wrongs don't make a right. And I'm still sorry if I gave you a concussion, Rodney." She looked at Gavin. "Now what?"

"Now we pack up all this nice outdoor gear, bundle up and start walking."

"Earlier you said it was impossible," Shelby pointed out.

"I don't think you could make it alone. The two of us together have a better chance, especially now that I found some clothes. Plus, it's daylight now. We'll get as far as we can get before dark, then camp. We have enough food and water to last a couple of days."

"Oh, so the big, strong male has to take care of little ol' me?"

"Have you had survival training?"

"Uh, no."

"Well, I have." Okay, so he'd watched a show about survivalists on the Discovery Channel. But he'd watched carefully and he'd learned a lot.

"We can't just leave Rodney here."

"Don't leave me," Rodney pleaded. "I'll freeze—starve!"

Gavin looked at Rodney tied up and squirming on the floor and felt a sudden, irrational compassion for the pathetic man. He'd seen men like Rodney in prison. So long as he had the upper hand, he was a tough guy. But faced with someone stronger, he collapsed into a groveling weakling. A little bully, the kind the bigger bullies preyed on.

Gavin had no intention of leaving Rodney here, not when his partner was still out there. The partner could come back, free Rodney, and the two of them would come after Gavin and Shelby, tracking them easily through the snow. But he decided to use Rodney's fear first.

He addressed Rodney. "We'll take you with us on one condition. Tell us who you are and who hired you. And don't lie. I used to be a cop, and I interrogated my fair share of creeps. I can smell a lie a mile off."

The man they'd been calling Rodney flashed a belligerent look at Gavin and remained silent.

"Maybe we *should* leave him here," Shelby said. But it was too late. Rodney had figured out they weren't going to kill him or leave him to freeze or become some bear's dinner, and he wasn't talking.

"It doesn't matter," Gavin said. "Your prints are on file in the national database computer. Mmm, bet you can taste that prison food now. Those pork chops, so hard and dry you could break a window with 'em? And those gray, watery mashed potatoes. My favorite."

"Maybe we could work a deal," Rodney said quickly.

"What kind of deal?"

"I'll tell you what I know. You let me go. I'll take my chances in the woods, on my own."

"You'd ambush us and slit our throats. Don't think so."

"I'll give you something for free, then. To show good will."

"Yeah?"

"Miss Shelby's worth more dead than alive. That's all I'm saying unless you untie me."

Gavin looked at Shelby. "Life insurance," he said. "Owen must have a big policy on you."

Shelby merely looked confused. "When Jake was born, Owen and I took out policies on each other. But we canceled both policies when we split up."

"Are you sure he canceled yours?"

"Pretty sure. Yes, I remember getting some notice in the mail to that effect. I think. Oh, shoot, I don't know for sure. Maybe that was the notice I received when I canceled *his* policy."

Rodney just flashed an unsettling grin.

Gavin knew he could break the guy if given enough time. But time wasn't a luxury they had right now. Anyway, it didn't matter. They already knew who was behind the kidnapping. This cabin was all the proof they needed. "Let's pack up and get going. We have a lot of miles to cover."

Chapter Ten

Shelby's legs burned after the first hour of slogging through the snow, and she was glad Gavin had stopped her from trying to make this descent on her own and in the dark. She'd probably be frozen in the middle of a snowdrift right now.

"How far do you think we've gone?" she asked Gavin. He and Rodney walked a few feet ahead of her. Gavin carried the backpack, filled with Clif bars and water. The lantern was attached to the outside of the pack, matches wrapped securely in several layers of plastic in an inside pocket. The sleeping bag was stacked on top of the pack.

"A couple of miles," Gavin said.

"Is that all?"

"Don't think about it. Enjoy the scenery. It's beautiful up here. I've never been to Colorado."

Shelby knew Gavin was just trying to buoy her spirits. They were still in dire straits. They didn't have enough food and water for three people. They had no shelter if they had to spend the night—and they would, unless the cabin wasn't as far into the wilderness as

Shelby remembered. Gavin said he thought he could get a fire started, so maybe they wouldn't freeze to death.

"How do your feet feel?" she asked. The ancient boots they'd found in the footlocker had been too small for Gavin. So he'd wrapped his running shoes in several layers of plastic packaging that had come off the camping supplies. He'd secured the plastic with duct tape, found in Rodney's jacket pocket. But that wasn't nearly enough protection.

"I can still feel my toes," Gavin replied.

"Rodney's got good boots. You two could trade them back and forth."

Rodney grumbled over that suggestion. Once he'd figured out they weren't going to let him go no matter what, he'd gotten very surly. Gavin had instructed Shelby to walk a few feet behind them, the gun in her purse, and to take out the gun and shoot to kill if Rodney tried anything. But she suspected Rodney knew she would have a very hard time pulling the trigger.

"I already thought of taking Rodney's shoes," Gavin said. "They're too small."

She worried he would get frostbite. And that old jacket of Owen's was hardly any protection.

Then there was Rodney, who didn't have a jacket at all. The ski bib would at least keep his torso warm, but a thin pair of gloves were all the protection he had for his hands.

Shelby was the only one with a hat. All in all, she was pretty well protected, thanks to Owen's free use of her credit card. She felt almost guilty that she wasn't colder.

She focused on the scenery, as Gavin had suggested. It *was* incredibly beautiful. They were very near the tree line, and through the surrounding woods she could see jagged granite peaks piercing the bright blue sky. Pine trees, some of them soaring a hundred feet, stood majestically in their snowy shrouds. It was eerily quiet, with only the sound of the snow crunching beneath their feet and the rustle of clothing breaking the silence.

Early in their trek, they'd been able to follow the truck's tire tracks. But blowing snow had soon obliterated the tracks, and now they weren't even a hundred percent sure they were still on the narrow, twisting road. They kept following what looked like the widest break in the trees. Sometimes the terrain was so steep they wound up descending on their butts.

Shelby half expected to find the truck in a ditch somewhere. She couldn't imagine how that unwieldy truck, never intended for snow, had traversed this treacherous path.

"There," Gavin said, pointing at something on the side of the road. It took Shelby a few moments to realize he was pointing at the remnants of a tire track. The truck had apparently skidded to the side of the road, then recovered.

Shelby was relieved. They hadn't wandered deeper into the woods, where they would march around in circles until they starved.

Her relief was short-lived. Rodney, who'd been quiet and cooperative for the past couple of hours, took advantage of their momentary distraction. He head butted Gavin, knocking him into a snowdrift, then took off running into the woods, leaping gazellelike through the deep snow, his long legs an advantage.

Gavin cursed and scrambled to his feet, giving chase.

But with his clumsy foot wrappings and his bruised and burned legs, Rodney soon outdistanced him.

Shelby ran a poor third behind the two men, fumbling to get the gun out of her purse. Once she had it, she fired a warning shot into the air. The blast was louder than she expected, echoing for several seconds around the mountains, and her hand tingled from the gun's kick.

But Rodney wasn't stopping. Gavin slowed, then stopped, leaning over and breathing hard, rubbing his bad leg.

"It's too late," he said. "That sucker's gone."

"Guess I wasn't much help. Me and my big, bad gun."

"Not much you could have done, besides shoot him in the back, and I wouldn't recommend it."

"He'll die out there," she said. "He has no food, no water, no sleeping bag…"

"It won't take him long to realize he made a tactical error," Gavin said. "He'll come crawling back."

The possibility was not in the least comforting. "Gavin, you take the gun. You're the one who's trained to use it, and we might need it to protect ourselves against Rodney if he comes back. I'm obviously useless." She held the small revolver out to him, but he still didn't take it.

"I won't go back to prison." His voice was low, quick.

"Gavin! These are special circumstances. Do you think I'd actually turn you in when I'm begging you to take the gun to protect me?"

Finally he saw the sense in what she was saying, and he took the gun. He took his gloves off, expertly checked the cylinder, then stuck the weapon in the waistband of his jeans at the small of his back.

"Let's press on," he said. "Keep your eyes open for Rodney."

The beauty of the scenery was lost on her after that. Every branch that snapped, every rustle of wind, made her jump, positive Rodney had come back to kill them. He'd said she was worth more dead than alive, so obviously killing her was what he'd had in mind. A carefully staged hiking accident. That meant double indemnity. If that insurance was still in effect, Owen would collect a cool half-million dollars.

If she had her way, Owen would find himself in a cold prison cell instead. She was over being shocked and saddened by what Owen had become. She was mad now, and she was going to nail him to the wall.

"Did you say something?" Gavin asked.

She probably had spoken aloud, she'd been so engrossed in her vengeful thoughts. "I was wondering when we should stop for lunch."

Gavin slowed his pace. "We've been on the go for a while. It must be close to noon. Let's dig in to those delicious Clif Bars."

"They're actually not bad," Shelby said. Off the side of the road they found an outcropping of rock to sit on. Gavin took off his pack, then handed Shelby a bottle of water.

"What flavor do you want?" he asked. "Peanut butter or cranberry?"

"I'll try the cranberry." She was weak from hunger and exertion, her leg muscles trembling, unused to this much and this type of exercise. She took off her gloves and ripped the wrapper off the nutrition bar. She ate it quickly, scarcely bothering to chew. A cheeseburger and french fries would have been better, but she was grateful for what she had.

"Want another?" Gavin asked.

She noticed he'd only eaten one. "Do we have enough for seconds?"

He shrugged. "If you're still hungry, eat."

"I'll split one with you." She didn't want him sacrificing his share of the food supply for her comfort. And suddenly she knew that was exactly what he would do, if she didn't nix it. She looked at him, at the sun shining on his uncompromising face, his eyes reflecting the blue of the sky and the green of the trees, and her heart did a funny little flip.

Abruptly she realized she saw in that face the qualities she'd always sought in a man, qualities she'd mistakenly believed Owen possessed—strength, determination, selflessness, compassion, even for a worm like Rodney. All wrapped up in a gorgeous body. It didn't seem to matter anymore that he was an ex-con, a former drug addict. Whatever circumstances had led him to cave in to a weakness, she knew it would never happen again. Few of the ex-cons she dealt with truly had the ability to learn from their mistakes.

Gavin did. Gavin was special. And she was a little worried that she might be falling in love with him.

GAVIN'S LEG FELT as if there was a knife twisting inside it. But he tried not to show his pain. Right now, the only thing that kept Shelby going was the confidence that they were going to survive. And the only reason she believed in their survival was because she was relying on him—his supposed superior knowledge of the wilderness, his supposed superior strength.

If he let his own confidence slip, even a little, he was afraid Shelby would fall apart. And with his own strength ebbing and the night closing in, he didn't know if he could keep himself together and her, too.

They needed each other to be strong.

The sun was setting behind the western peaks, now.

"We should stop and make camp," he said, forcing optimism into his voice.

"I thought for sure we'd find something or some person by now," Shelby said dejectedly. "Maybe just a little farther?"

"Dark will come quickly once the sun is behind the mountains. And then it'll get cold—fast. I want to build a fire before my hands get too cold." He also wanted to choose a campsite carefully, where they would have the best chance of spotting Rodney before he could get close enough to strike.

"Okay. Guess I was just hoping we wouldn't have to sleep in the open."

"It won't be too bad. You've got the sleeping bag. It's a good one."

"And how are you supposed to keep warm?"

"I'll be okay. Let's get off the road and back into the trees, where we'll be protected some from the wind." No sense advertising their whereabouts to Rodney. He'd have no trouble following their tracks, if he had a mind to. But at least he wouldn't be able to spot the fire from miles away.

They hiked into the woods about a quarter mile until Gavin found a site to his liking. A cliff with a slight overhang would protect them from the elements and provide a natural barrier to predators—animal and human alike. They would only have to keep watch on three sides instead of four. The site had the added attraction of a partially fallen pine tree. The trunk had snapped about three feet up and had fallen to the ground at an angle. He wouldn't even need to build a frame for a lean-to—which he couldn't, anyway, since his only tool was the rusty kitchen knife.

For the fire, he gathered some bigger logs to make a platform. Then he ripped some good-size branches off the underside of the fallen pine tree. They were good and dry, and he figured they'd burn fast and hot. He crisscrossed these in a pattern he remembered from the TV show, then filled in with smaller branches, and finally with some dry moss. The last thing he added were the wrappers from their Clif Bars.

"So that's what you were saving those for," Shelby said. "I'm impressed. This looks so professional."

"Save your praise for after I get the thing started."

He had a couple dozen matches. With Shelby blocking the wind, he ignited the paper wrappers, then the moss, and fed the tiny blaze small twigs. Finally the larger branches caught, and he figured he was home free.

He showed Shelby, who'd never been camping in her life, how to tend the fire. Then he went to work gathering evergreen boughs and leaning them up against the fallen tree trunk. He lined the floor with small, green pine branches and leaves, for insulation.

When he returned to Shelby and the fire, the blaze was burning a bit hotter and brighter than he was hoping. "Don't add more wood for a while. No sense making ourselves too visible."

He dragged one final log close to the fire, for seating, and he and Shelby sank onto it. They said nothing for a long time. It was almost dark now, and the woods started to hum with the sounds of the night—wind in the treetops, an owl and something a little more unsettling—the howl of an animal.

"There aren't any wolves in this part of Colorado," he said when Shelby shot him an alarmed look.

"You don't even know what part of Colorado we're in!"

"It's probably a dog—or a coyote. Anyway, the fire will keep animals away."

"What about when we're sleeping?"

But Gavin didn't answer. A movement in his peripheral vision had caught his attention. He scanned the darkening woods, his hand already on the small revolver.

He sagged with relief when he saw that it was only a small animal—a bird of some kind, a wild turkey or a pheasant, maybe. They'd probably disturbed it from its roost with all their tree shaking.

"What is it?" Shelby whispered.

"Dinner." He raised the gun and aimed carefully, not wanting to waste a bullet. He slowly squeezed the trigger.

"No!" Shelby grabbed his arm just as he fired. The shot went wild, and the bird took flight and disappeared.

"Shelby! What'd you go and do that for?"

"You were going to kill a bird?"

"Yeah. It's called hunting. I'm starving, aren't you? We've got this nice fire, and nothing to cook."

Shelby just kept staring at him, her blue eyes big and

sad. "I could never have eaten it," she finally said. "Poor thing."

"Poor thing? What about poor us?"

"We've got Clif Bars."

"You're not a vegetarian, are you?"

"Well, no."

"What exactly do you think goes into your Big Mac? Don't you think about the poor cow?"

"That's different."

"So you don't mind eating meat as long as someone else does your dirty work and hides it from you."

"All right, so I'm a hypocrite. You're right, I should have let you kill Woodsy Owl. This is about survival, not my sensibilities."

"It was a turkey, I think," he said quietly.

"Do you even know how to clean a turkey?"

"Sure." He'd have figured it out, at any rate. Damn, he could almost taste those roasted turkey legs.

"I'm sorry," she said. "You can have my last Clif bar if you want."

He put an arm around her. "It's okay. We won't starve." He left his arm there, and she snuggled up against him. With the crackling fire and the beautiful, snowy woods all around them, the situation would have been almost pleasant if they'd had more food—and a king-size bed with an electric blanket.

Suddenly something crashed into the fire from above. There was a lot of sizzle and steam, and the fire was extinguished in a heartbeat. They were plunged into darkness.

"What happened?" Shelby asked, alarmed.

Gavin was afraid he knew. A huge, green branch

laden with snow had come from above them—and it hadn't arrived under its own power. The gun was already in his hand as he stood and listened.

A twig cracked. He felt rather than saw the man coming at him out of the darkness. Something whooshed right next to his face. His attacker had a club, maybe a log, and had just missed Gavin's head.

In a split second, Gavin saw the possibilities spread out before him. If the club found its target next time, Gavin would be stunned—or dead. And Shelby would be defenseless. Faced with a choice between harm to Shelby and his worst nightmare—return to prison—he knew he would protect the woman like a wild animal protecting its mate. To save Shelby, he would disregard the fact he'd been forbidden to ever touch a gun. For her, he was prepared to kill.

He saw something moving. Or he thought he did. He reached behind him with his left hand and caught Shelby, just to be sure he knew where she was.

"I've got a gun and I'll shoot to kill," he said, just in case the attacker wasn't Rodney and didn't know he'd ambushed someone who was armed.

Gavin felt the rush of air as the man made a flying leap toward him. They both went down. Desperate hands grappled for the gun. Shelby screamed. The anguished sound was punctuated by the loud pop of the gun, partially muffled by the two men on top of it.

Chapter Eleven

"Gavin? Gavin?" Shelby cried. "For God's sake, say something."

"I'm okay, I think," Gavin said, and Shelby nearly wept with relief.

She stood still, afraid to move in the darkness. "What happened? Is someone else here?"

"Someone else *was* here." She heard some scraping and shuffling. "Where's the backpack? And the lantern?"

"Here, I've got the backpack. Not sure where the lantern went." She stooped down and felt around her feet, found the log they'd been sitting on. Had the lantern been sitting on the log? "Wait, here it is." She held out both the backpack and the lantern in the direction of Gavin's voice, and he took them.

More rustling. Then the strike of a match. Some fumbling, and then the lantern blazed with its cheerful light.

That was when Shelby saw Rodney, not three feet away from where she was standing. Eyes glazed over, blood in the snow beneath his head—so much blood.

She opened her mouth, but no sound came out. She

had no air in her lungs with which to scream. She turned away from the gory sight and faced the rock wall.

"Damn," Gavin muttered. "I knew you shouldn't have given me the gun." His voice trailed off. His footsteps crunched in the snow as he walked away from the body, away from death.

That was when Shelby knew she had to pull herself together. Gavin had just killed a man. That was a lot to deal with. He didn't need her hysterics on top of everything else.

"If I hadn't given you the gun," she said, still not turning around but speaking loud enough that she was sure he could hear, "we'd both be dead right now." Then she made herself turn. She looked, not at the body, but at Gavin, who'd walked just to the edge of their little clearing, almost beyond the lantern glow.

Taking the long way around the ruined fire, so she wouldn't have to step over Rodney, she went to Gavin. Without hesitation, she put her arms around him.

"You had to do it," she said. "You saved our lives, and that's what matters. Survival."

"They train you for this stuff when you go to cop school," he said quietly, "but then they say you can't really prepare for it, that you can't know what it feels like until you do it. They were right."

"We'll bury him," Shelby said brightly. "We'll just bury him in the snow, way out here, away from our shelter. Then we'll go to sleep, and at first light we'll hike out of here, we'll find a town or a person or a car, and the nightmare will be over."

"You're not suggesting we don't *tell* anyone, are you?"

"No, no, of course not." That was exactly what she'd

been thinking, but she realized now that was insane. They had to go to some law-enforcement authorities and tell the whole horrible story so that Owen could be caught and put away. "We'll go straight to the sheriff in Peavy, or wherever."

"Then we shouldn't move him. We should leave the crime scene as pure as possible."

"Screw the crime scene. We can't just leave him there overnight. We have to think about...animals."

Gavin grimaced. "Right. Let's get it over with, then."

Shelby just closed off her mind to the horror as they dragged the body a hundred feet into the woods. With his hands, Gavin dug an indentation in the snow. They placed the body into it and heaped more snow on top until Rodney's white, waxy face and gaping mouth were no longer visible. With his pocketknife, Gavin marked a tree near the makeshift grave. Then they plodded back to the clearing.

There was still blood everywhere. Almost in a frenzy, Shelby kicked snow over the spots of red until they were completely obliterated. Then she ran back into the woods and retched, though there was very little in her stomach.

Gavin was beside her instantly. "You okay?"

She nodded and washed her mouth out with snow. "Can we go to bed now? Can we just go to sleep? I'm so tired I can't even think anymore."

They crawled into the fallen-tree lean-to, which was surprisingly cozy, dragging the sleeping bag with them. They piled their jackets on the floor of the shelter to make a bed, then unzipped the sleeping bag and used it as a blanket.

Shelby didn't think she could ever be warm and comfortable again. But with Gavin's body heat next to her, her shivering gradually subsided. She snuggled closer to him, and he put both arms around her.

"When Manny Cruz killed himself in my cubicle, his head exploded," she said, then wondered what on earth had made her say such a horrible thing.

Gavin stroked her hair and said nothing.

"His brains were on me," she continued, unable to stop. "I showered and showered, with the water so hot it burned me, but I never really felt like I could get him off me."

Gavin still said nothing.

"I never saw a dead person before that," she said. "I couldn't get the pictures out of my head. Every time I closed my eyes, there he was. And even though they cleaned my office really good and got me all new furniture, I couldn't sit at my desk without seeing him. And a week later, when I was typing a report, I saw this little fleck of red on my mouse. It was about the size of a pinhead. But I knew what it was, and I ran to the bathroom and threw up."

"Oh, Shelby."

"I just had no idea death was so ugly. And I should be saying comforting things to you right now, because I know you feel terrible about what happened, but I'm having flashbacks or something." She'd tried not to look, but she'd seen the exit wound in the back of Rodney's head, what was left of it, when they'd buried him.

"I've seen death before," Gavin said gruffly. "I'm a cop. I don't need comforting."

But he did. She knew he did. He was just being strong

and stoic, as he'd been from the beginning of this ordeal, and all for her sake.

She knew then for sure that she was falling in love with him.

When she'd first acknowledged her attraction to Gavin, she'd assumed it was his bad-boy appeal. Apparently there was a sinister part of her personality that was drawn to men with a dark side, she'd decided. Men like Owen, who didn't want to play by the rules. Well, she'd had her bad boy and it had been a colossal mistake; she wasn't going to repeat it.

Now she realized it wasn't Gavin's darkness that drew her. It was his strength, his goodness, his honor. Yes, he'd made mistakes. He undeniably had a dark side. But he'd taken responsibility for those mistakes rather than trying to blame others, society or his mother. And he'd undertaken the monumental task of reforming himself.

That was what she was falling in love with.

She wept against his shoulder as he held her, unquestioningly. Then, in their cocoon of crunching pine needles and down-filled nylon, he made love to her, so gently, with so much care, that she wanted to weep again with the sheer wonder of it.

SHELBY'S EVEN BREATHING told Gavin that she was asleep. Lord knew she needed it, probably more than the sex. He could use some sleep, too. But he was too tense, too shocked by what had just happened—all of it—to find the blissful escape of sleep.

He couldn't believe he and Shelby had made love. If he'd had any sense, he would have resisted the lure of Shelby's soft body and her obvious invitation.

He had, at first. As she'd clung to him, her head tucked in the crook of his neck, breathing close to his ear, her leg thrown over his, he'd tried very hard to ignore her. She'd been in a state of shock and in no condition to make decisions of any kind. But her hands had found the buttons on his flannel shirt and she'd started to undo them, one by one, her hands brushing tantalizingly against his bare chest.

He'd tried to stop her, knowing she probably wasn't thinking straight. It was a natural reaction to seek oblivion after a traumatic event. He'd also known with almost near certainty that she would regret having sex with him. So he'd stilled her hands, pulled them away from his bare skin, tucked them next to her own body with a little pat.

But she'd given a little sob and said one word. "Please."

That one word had undone him. How could he deny the tentative seduction of such a woman as Shelby Dorset, when for weeks he'd been practically paralyzed with wanting her?

And so he'd taken her, hoping he could give her some small measure of solace to blot out the evening's brutality. Hoping he could find some solace himself. He'd undressed her gently, as if she were an antique bisque doll that might crack with the slightest jar. She shivered with the cold, and he pressed the length of his body along hers until the tremors stopped. Then he'd kissed her softly, each kiss a question, an opportunity for her to turn her head and change her mind.

But she hadn't changed her mind, and Gavin hadn't found the strength to change it for her. And so he'd buried himself in her soft warmth, pulling her to him even more tightly, feeling her against every inch of his shaft, every angle and plane of his entire body. And for those few, brief moments when they were one, he felt a merging with her that rocked him to his core.

Now, bodies separated but still naked, he held her as she slept and felt utterly undeserving of what she'd given him.

He'd killed a man, which meant there was a very good chance he would be returning to prison. Granted, there had never been a more clear-cut case of self-defense. But would the authorities believe his version of what happened? Were the circumstances enough to warrant his possessing a gun in the first place? The Texas penal system could be fickle, and that was giving it some.

At some point, Gavin did manage to sleep. When his eyes fluttered open some time later, it was to the welcome glow of dawn—and Shelby, propped up on her elbows, watching him.

"Good morning," she said, and she was wearing a dopey smile that did something strange to the inside of his chest. "We made it. We survived the night."

"In spectacular fashion," he added, almost managing a smile of his own. Gavin had imagined waking up to Shelby furtively dragging on her clothes, avoiding his gaze, speaking only when necessary. He'd imagined her being mortified over her behavior the night before, maybe giving him some pretty little speech about how she hadn't been herself and that she didn't want to speak of it ever again.

The last thing he could have imagined was waking to Shelby's smile, her expression warm and open, her eyes shining even in the dim light.

"Did you sleep much?" she asked.

"A little. Mostly I listened to you sleeping."

She caught her breath. "Did I snore?"

"No. You breathe in a very ladylike fashion. How do you feel?"

"A darn sight better than I did last night. My grandmother used to always say everything looks better in the morning. I think she was right. I've never felt more alive than I do right now. For the first time in a couple of days, I know with absolute certainty that we're going to live. We're going to survive this thing, and we're going to be better, stronger people because of it. Do you believe me?"

He sighed. "I'll try, Shelby. But you're not the one facing going back to prison."

"No way," she scoffed. "These were special circumstances. No one will blame you for anything. Lord, Gavin, don't you get it? You're not the perp here. You're a hero. You saved my life as well as your own, and I'll cut down anyone who says otherwise."

He could almost believe her. From somewhere, he summoned a smile. "Okay, I'm a hero. But just remember this, Mary Sunshine. No one's going to believe my version of what happened."

"But they'll believe me."

"Yes. Which makes you the one thing standing between me and a four-by-four prison cell for the rest of my life. Your reputation, your impeccable background—that's what'll save my bacon. There's just one thing…." He hated to even bring it up. But it had to be said.

"What is it, Gavin?"

"You can't let anyone know we made love."

She looked at him, perplexed. "Not that I was planning to go blabbing to every person on the street, but what does that have to do with anything?"

"The fact we've been lovers, even briefly, throws your story into question. They'll think you're lying to protect me because we're involved, somehow. If anyone finds out you slept with an ex-con, one of your parolees, your reputation goes out the window—and so do my chances of staying on the outside."

"I see."

"Do you?"

She sighed. "Yes, I think I do."

Shelby was considerably less cheerful as they broke camp and prepared to trek back through the woods to the road.

AFTER TWO HOURS OF TRUDGING, they hit a main road, where tire ruts told them vehicles had been out and about since the last snow. Another fifteen minutes, and an SUV lumbered toward them, heading down the mountain.

Not taking any chances, Gavin stood in the middle of the road and waved his arms. When the SUV slowed, he walked to the driver's window and flashed his most winning smile at the driver, an older man with a wild salt-and-pepper beard.

"Man, are we glad to see you. We got stranded in our cabin. Snowed in. We're out of food and almost out of water."

"The weather up here can surprise you if you're not used to it," the driver said with a knowing grin. "Hop in."

Gavin had never been so glad to see the inside of a

vehicle in his life. He rode in front with the bearded man, but first he helped Shelby into the back seat. She was so tired from walking through the thick snow that her legs trembled. She could scarcely hoist herself up to the high seat. But she hadn't complained of being sore or tired, not once.

His own legs weren't in much better shape.

Gavin and Shelby had agreed not to tell anyone their story until they reached a law-enforcement-type person. They didn't want to scare anyone, or convince a potential Good Samaritan that he didn't want to become involved.

Gavin made small-talk with the bearded man about freak blizzards, enjoying the warm air blasting from the truck's heater. He casually asked the man to drop them at the nearest police department or sheriff's office.

"I'm heading to Seton," the man said. "Peavy's closer, but I don't think they have any law in Peavy."

"Seton's fine," Shelby said.

Twenty minutes later, they found themselves facing a square-jawed sheriff who, if he'd lived in the South, would undoubtedly have been called Bubba or Billy-Bob. As it was, his name was Ruston P. Shanks, and he obviously didn't like strangers in his town. Gavin had grave misgivings about confiding in him, but they didn't have much choice.

He let Shelby do the telling, but even from her, the story sounded far-fetched. Gavin knew that, had he been the one sitting on the other side of the desk, he'd have had doubts right away.

Shelby's monologue was peppered liberally with interruptions from the Sheriff such as, "You escaped *how?*" and "You never met this man before?" When she got to the part where Rodney attacked them, she faltered and her eyes glistened with tears. He resisted the urge to take her hand or reveal any tenderness. Now, more than ever, it seemed important that they show no intimacy in front of the skeptical sheriff.

He was about to jump in and take over the story when Shelby blurted out, "I killed the man, Sheriff Ruston. I believed he was intent on killing us, and I shot at him with the gun. I didn't mean to kill him, I just wanted him to stop his attack. But I've never handled a gun before, and it was dark, and I panicked, and the man ended up dead."

Gavin was so shocked he just sat there, frozen. He opened his mouth to refute what she'd just said, but she shot him a look that warned, *Don't you dare say a word.* And then he realized she'd planned the lie all along, because she'd left out the part of the story where she'd insisted he take the gun from her.

And then the opportunity to object was lost, because Sheriff Shanks had suddenly become a lot more animated. He did everything but jump up and shout, "Hot damn! A murder in my county!" And Gavin realized that if he refuted Shelby's statement, if he accused her of lying, she ceased to be his unimpeachable witness.

After Shelby assured the sheriff that, yes, she could take them back to where they'd buried the dead man, he disappeared for a few minutes, leaving them alone.

"I can't believe this," he muttered to Shelby. "I really can't. Do you have any idea what you've done, telling a lie?"

"I won't risk your going back to prison," she retorted,

keeping her voice low. "They might suspect you of murder, but no one would suspect me."

"And if they want you to take a polygraph? Did you think of that?"

By the look on her face, she hadn't.

"Look, Shelby, I appreciate your wanting to protect me. But lying to an officer of the law is a bad, bad idea. When Sheriff Bubba comes back, I'm setting the record straight, and you better back me up."

"I can't turn back now. Just let it be. I can keep the story straight."

"And what if they test my hands or my jacket sleeve for gunshot residue?"

"Why would they?"

"Because the whole story sounds fishy. Look, Beau Maddox lied to protect me when I was arrested. He said I had the gun in my hand, but I hadn't pointed it at him. The truth is, I fired that gun."

Shelby's face went pale. "You did?"

"I hit the barn wall well above Beau's head. I wasn't trying to kill him, just prove I was serious about not being captured. Or, hell, maybe I was trying to provoke him into shooting me, which I did. Anyway, he lied so it wouldn't look so bad, and I let him, and I've never felt right about it. I won't repeat that mistake."

"Gavin, think about it."

But she wouldn't change his mind. And when the Sheriff returned to his desk, Gavin told him the true story. "Shelby had only honorable intentions, Sheriff Shanks," Gavin said. "She was trying to protect me. I'm out on parole, and she doesn't want to see me go back to jail."

The sheriff turned laser-sharp eyes on Shelby. "Why would he go to jail if he shot a man in self-defense?"

"I was afraid no one would believe him," Shelby said. "He didn't even want to handle the gun, because he's serious about following the provisions of his parole. I made him take the gun, and he ended up shooting someone because of me, and I just feel very responsible for the whole thing."

The sheriff looked from one of them to the other, re-assessing the situation. Then he refocused on Shelby. "What exactly is the nature of your relationship with Mr. Schuyler? Aside from being his parole officer."

"Former parole officer," she clarified. Then she said, with perfect candor, "Our relationship isn't platonic, but beyond that, I honestly can't tell you."

Gavin closed his eyes. *Now* she decides to tell the truth. They were in serious trouble.

"Mebbe we better go find that boy you buried in the snow," the sheriff said. "Then we'll figure out what to do about it."

So they rode in the back seat of a county-owned four-wheel-drive SUV, past Peavy and up the mountain road, up the smaller mountain road. Gavin instructed the sheriff to stop when they reached a particular outcropping of rocks.

"We have to hike in from here."

Shelby stayed in the vehicle while Gavin trudged through the snow with the sheriff and two deputies, who'd followed in a separate car. Following his and Shelby's footprints back to their campsite was no problem. He found the tree he'd marked and the makeshift grave.

One of the sheriff's deputies poked around in the

snow. "Yup, there's a body here all right. Better call the coroner and the crime-scene guys."

SHELBY KEPT TRYING to make the blockheaded Colorado State Trooper understand that she was the victim. But from the time Rodney's body had been unearthed, the tone of their encounter with the Blair County Sheriff's Department had changed. She and Gavin had been separated and questioned separately about the events of the past two days, first by the sheriff and whatever deputies thought it might be fun to take shots at them, then by the Colorado State Patrol, which had apparently been consulted when the scope of the crime became more than the tiny sheriff's department could handle. They allowed her to make a phone call, and her first thought was to check on Jake. But she reached Owen's voice mail. She quickly dialed again, this time opting for Rosie. Her friend was probably worried sick about her. But Rosie wasn't home, either, and her cell was off. Where was everyone?

As a last resort, Shelby called her parents. No luck. She was forced to leave what was probably a confusing message.

All in all, Shelby was questioned for more than five hours. She'd been given nothing to eat, and water to drink only when she'd insisted. Finally, she'd decided she'd had enough and had declared she wouldn't say another word without legal counsel. Clearly she was being considered a suspect.

Once they were sure she knew where she stood, the gloves came off. "We'd sure rather have your cooperation," the state trooper, her latest tormenter, said.

"What do you think you've had for the past six hours?" she snapped. "I want a lawyer and I want one now."

She couldn't make it any clearer. And unless they wanted to be accused of violating her constitutional rights, they had to stop badgering her—which they did. Instead, they placed her under arrest.

Chapter Twelve

Gavin used his one phone call to contact Ace McCullough. If anyone could cut through the bull, Ace could.

He didn't know whom Shelby had called, or even if she'd been arrested, or where she was, for that matter. He hadn't seen her since before noon, when he'd been escorted to one sheriff's vehicle and she to another. No one would tell him anything.

When they'd tried to hustle him into an interrogation room, he'd flatly refused to talk to anyone without a lawyer. He knew how this game worked because he'd played on both sides. He didn't even give them the opportunity to tell him they were his friends, that they only wanted to help him, that by refusing to cooperate he was casting himself in a negative light. He told them he'd been a police detective, and they left him alone—in a basement holding cell at the county jail.

At least they'd fed him. The food wasn't even all that bad. Then again, after a steady diet of Clif Bars, anything different would have tasted good.

At nine o'clock that night, a guard opened his cell door and escorted Gavin to a magistrate's chambers on the second floor, where an attorney he'd never seen before had a thirty-second conversation with him, ascertaining that he most certainly wanted to plead innocent to any wrongdoing.

The legal proceeding lasted about three minutes. His bail was set at twenty-five thousand dollars, and he was led back to his cell.

At midnight, Gavin had just bedded down on his hard-as-a-rock cot, trying not to think about the fact that he was behind bars. He focused on being grateful he was alive and reasonably warm and well fed. He'd figure out the rest tomorrow, after he got some sleep.

But sleep wasn't to be. The cell door clanged open. "Heads up," the guard said. "You've been sprung."

Ace McCullough was waiting for him, grinning. "You promised me when I hired you that you wouldn't get into trouble." But there was no sting in the words.

"Where's Shelby?" Gavin asked right away.

"Don't worry, she's been sprung, too."

"Then she was arrested?"

"Three people in the woods, one of them dead, the other two climbing all over each other to take credit for the deed. What were these local-yokel cops supposed to do?"

"How about believe us when we told them it was self-defense? Please tell me they didn't send Mutt and Jeff to work the crime scene."

"They sent good people," Ace assured him as Gavin got his jacket, gloves and the backpack returned to him. "Just one little problem. It appears your friend in the woods was shot in the back of the head."

Gavin froze. *"What?"*

"That's what I hear. Execution style."

"That was an exit wound, I'm sure of it," Gavin said. "I think the bullet must have gone through his neck."

"What about the ligature marks around his wrists?" Ace asked.

"Those we explained. *He* was going to kill *us*. Binding his hands was the only way we could get him down the mountain. And in the end, it wasn't enough to contain him."

Ace laid a hand on Gavin's shoulder as they headed out into the cold, cold night. "We'll get it straightened out. I've hired a good attorney friend of mine to handle this. He'll be here in the morning."

"Then who was that lawyer who appeared with me earlier?"

Ace grinned. "Shelby is responsible for him. Now, if I was up on a murder charge, don't know that I would have called my ex-husband to handle things, but—"

Gavin cursed extravagantly. "Did you say her ex-husband? That lawyer was Owen Dorset?"

Ace nodded.

"Ace, where is Shelby now?" Gavin tried not to sound as anxious as he felt.

"She's staying at a little hotel in town, and that's where we're headed, too."

"We need to make sure she's safe. We think Owen Dorset is the one behind the kidnapping."

"Oh. Well, that explains your agitation. Maybe you better sit down and tell me the whole story."

"As soon as I see that Shelby is safe."

IT WAS A TEN-MINUTE DRIVE into the quaint town of Seton, the Blair County seat. Ace pulled his rental car into a spot in front of the Silver Queen Hotel, a three-story brick structure at least a hundred years old on a picturesque street Gavin might have appreciated under better circumstances. He hardly waited for the car to come to a stop before bolting out the door and barreling through the hotel's entrance, intent on finding Shelby if he had to take the building down brick by brick.

Fortunately, he didn't have to. Shelby was sitting in the lobby waiting for him. She jumped up when she saw him, and Gavin had to stop himself from running to her and crushing her against him.

She looked as if she wanted to do more than just stand there, too. But they were both aware of the hotel clerk's curious observation, so they didn't even touch each other.

"How are you?" Gavin asked inanely.

"Really angry at the way we've been treated. Scared to death. Worried about what was happening to you." She nodded toward Ace, who'd flopped in an overstuffed red-velvet chair and propped his feet up on an antique coffee table, looking as if he figured this conversation might go on for a while. "After Owen got me out, I insisted he take care of you, too. Did he?"

"Oddly enough, yes." Gavin lowered his voice so the clerk wouldn't be able to hear. "What the hell is Owen doing here? You picked a strange person to call for help."

"*I* didn't call him. I called my father. He wasn't home and I left a message—probably a rather confused-sounding one—about where I was and that I'd been charged with a crime and needed a lawyer. It didn't occur to me that he would turn the matter over to Owen, of all people! I almost fainted when I saw him."

"What did you say?"

"I played dumb, like I didn't suspect his involvement. I didn't tell him the whole story, and he didn't ask. He was in a bit of a rush—he has to be in court in the morning. So we just went before the magistrate, pled innocent, he paid my five thousand bail—"

"Five thousand! They set mine at twenty-five," Gavin grumbled.

"He said he would take care of you, too, but I wasn't sure if he really would. Then I ran into Ace, and he said he would pay your bond and meet me back here. We're not allowed to leave town, just like in some old Western movie."

"So Owen's gone?" Gavin asked, just to be sure.

"Said he was flying back home tonight. My mother is taking care of Jake, thank God."

Gavin sank into one of the lobby's plush chairs, almost sick with relief.

"It's late," Ace said. "The best thing you two can do for yourselves is get a good night's sleep. Oliver Houseman will be here in the morning."

"Oliver Houseman?" Gavin and Shelby said together. He was the best criminal lawyer in Payton, possibly in all of East Texas.

"Hey, I don't mess around. Gavin, the cases are piling up on your desk. I need you back." Ace stood and pulled a hotel key from his pocket, handing it to Gavin. "I already got you a room. Second floor, next to Shelby's." He winked. "I'm on three. See you kids in the morning, about eight."

He sauntered to the old-fashioned cage elevator.

Gavin visually examined Shelby, just to be sure she was really okay, that the cops hadn't used a rubber hose on her. She looked as if she'd bathed and washed her hair. She wore different clothes. He, on the other hand, was a grubby mess. Even if he thought Shelby would welcome his touch, he couldn't stand the idea of inflicting his lack of hygiene on her.

More to the point, he didn't have a clue whether she wanted any further intimacy with him. When they'd been in the grip of a crazy guy with a gun, fearful for their lives, they'd naturally clung together. He'd read of studies that showed how shared danger—even something as mild as riding a roller coaster or crossing a rickety-looking bridge—drew people together sexually. Now that the immediate physical danger was over, did Shelby regret her actions? Was she embarrassed that she'd come on to him?

He still felt as if he'd taken advantage of the situation, though he knew of few men who wouldn't have caved in his place.

"I guess we should turn in," he finally said.

"Yeah. Tomorrow's going to be a long day."

They walked to the elevator, pushed the call button, waited silently as the lift lumbered down from the third floor. Gavin opened the cage and they stepped inside.

"Did they interrogate you?" he asked.

"For five hours. I know that was dumb on my part. But I felt like I had to make them understand. In the end I just made the situation worse."

"Did you tell them your suspicions about Owen?"

"No. I figured that could come later, when some responsible agency actually investigates the crime. The real crime. I was just focusing on the facts."

The elevator jerked to a stop, and they stepped out. "Gavin, there's something I don't understand. I know Rodney was shot in the head, but they say it was execution style. That's not possible, is it?"

He shook his head. "It was dark, and we were wrestling for the gun and it went off. I can't swear to exactly what happened. But the idiot cops are wrong, and the autopsy will tell the tale."

She nodded.

Gavin looked at his key. "My room's right here."

"Mine's just there." She pointed to the next door down. Then, abruptly, she threw her arms around his neck and kissed him, quickly, almost furtively, before releasing him just as suddenly and scurrying to her room. She was locked safely behind her door before Gavin could even process what had happened.

He wouldn't have thought he could find a reason to smile, given the grim circumstances, but he was grinning like an idiot as he unlocked his own door.

The small room had a brass bed with a patchwork quilt, an oak nightstand and dresser, and an armoire. Compared to his jail cell, it was princely quarters.

Sitting on the bed was a bag from Wal-Mart. Inside was a fresh set of clothes and some essential toiletries, and a bottle of Percodan.

Bless Ace. Gavin took a long, hot bath, shaved off his three days' worth of beard, and finally crawled between crisp, faintly scented cotton sheets. He didn't need the painkillers—he was asleep before his head hit the pillow.

THE SILVER QUEEN HOTEL had its own little restaurant, where the coffee was strong and brewed from freshly ground beans. The food was good, too. Ace consumed a mountain of pancakes. Shelby ordered a Denver omelet and ate every scrap, including the hash browns, toast and orange juice that came with it. She would never take food for granted again.

Gavin seemed to enjoy his meal, as well, and he looked a hundred percent better than he had yesterday with his freshly shaven face. The purpling bruises and cuts on the side of his head from where Rodney had hit him with the log were more visible now, she noticed. Plus, he was still bruised and cut up from his encounter with the truck bumper—all evidence to back up their claims that they'd only been defending themselves against a crazed assailant. But it pained Shelby to see Gavin so battered. He claimed the injuries no longer hurt, but she didn't believe him.

As their waitress cleared the dishes, Oliver Houseman entered the hotel dining room, and every eye in the place was on him. He was, indeed, a commanding presence as he walked over to their table and shook hands with everyone.

Houseman was African-American, in his late forties, tall and fit and handsome. If they ever did a movie of his life, Denzel Washington could easily portray him. His smile showed even, white teeth. Shelby liked him instantly, and as he got down to business, she felt immeasurably more optimistic about her defense. He had an uncanny ability to focus on the pertinent facts, to coax her and Gavin into remembering details that could help them. Though the story was hopelessly convoluted, he understood the implications immediately, never doubted they were telling the truth.

Once he felt he had a complete picture, Oliver got on his cell phone, contacting investigators in Payton to check out parts of the story. He had them looking for Gavin's car, which he'd abandoned in a ditch. He had them talking to people at the grocery store and the doughnut shop where Shelby had stopped just before her kidnapping. Then he applied pressure to the local law, making sure they carefully examined Owen's fishing cabin, doing his own interrogation about what they'd looked for at the scene of Rodney's shooting. He even had investigators contacting truck-rental companies in and around Payton. These were all jobs the police should have been doing, but he wasn't leaving anything to chance.

Watching Oliver Houseman operate was a thing of beauty.

Once he'd covered the bases on the phone, he took some Polaroid snapshots of Gavin's injuries, then left them, promising he was off to rattle some cages in person. Ace left, too, confident they were in good hands.

It felt odd, suddenly having nothing to do. Shelby drained her fifth cup of coffee, totally wired from caffeine.

"What do you want to do?" Shelby asked Gavin. She'd already called her mother and talked to Jake, reassuring him that she would be home soon. She'd had to struggle not to cry from the relief of hearing his voice.

"Oliver said the preliminary autopsy results wouldn't be released until this afternoon. I can't just sit around waiting, I'll go crazy."

"Let's go for a walk," Gavin suggested.

After all their hiking the past couple of days, Shelby had thought she'd never willingly walk anywhere again. But getting out and working the stiffness out of her limbs sounded good. They got their jackets and gloves and headed out into the bright winter day to see what Seton, Colorado, had to offer.

It was a beautiful little town that had grown up around a silver mine. After the mine was played out, the town had almost died. Then some enterprising soul had opened a ski resort, and tourism had come to the rescue. The main street was picture-postcard pretty now, with restaurants and antiques shops and a museum and even a movie theater.

They ambled along the sidewalks, peering in windows, sometimes entering a shop to warm up and look at the knickknacks for sale. No one took them for anything but ordinary tourists, and the sheer normalcy of it all made Shelby want to giggle. Two days ago they'd been stranded on a mountain under attack by a crazed killer. Yesterday they'd been jailed for murder. Today they were sipping hot chocolate and trying on silly-looking hand-knitted caps at a craft shop.

They had lunch at a little hamburger place, where Shelby once again ate every crumb of food on her plate, even the dill-pickle spear.

When the table was cleared and she'd paid the check—Gavin's wallet had gone missing somewhere—

she reached over and took his hand, evidently surprising him, judging from the look on his face.

Why was he so surprised? she wondered. After all they'd been through the past few days, she felt closer to him than she had any human other than her son.

"I missed you yesterday," she said. "And last night. I've gotten kind of used to having you around."

"We made a pretty good team out there," he agreed, folding his hand around her fingertips.

Why was he talking in the past tense? She'd thought he wanted to be with her. Last night, she'd lain awake listening to the old pipes shriek as Gavin had bathed, and she'd thought he would come to her when he was finished. When he hadn't, she'd reminded herself that they were both exhausted. They needed sleep, not sex. But today, when they were rested and fed and clean and safe…

"Gavin, we need to talk about what happened between us."

He wouldn't meet her gaze. "We don't have to, if you don't want to. We were under duress, Shelby. I'm not going to throw it back in your face. It never would have happened under normal circumstances."

"Oh." Her chest felt as if a balloon had just deflated inside it. "I see."

"We're facing a murder charge. You've never been charged with a crime. You don't know what it's like. We'll need every ounce of energy and attention we have in us to fight it. That doesn't leave time for having an affair, or a fling, or whatever you want to call it."

"I see," she said again, snatching her hand out of his. An affair? A *fling?* What an awful thing to say. She could have cheerfully poured the rest of her Coke over his head.

"Don't take this wrong, Shelby. I don't believe you're thinking straight right now. You're scared, you're under pressure, and I'm your only port in a storm. But when we come out of this thing—and we will—I don't want you to have regrets. It's not that I don't want you. Believe me, I do. But I'm trying to get some perspective, and you should, too."

Shelby bit her lip. He could use all the pretty words he wanted, but she recognized a brush-off when she heard one.

She'd been totally naive, thinking he would automatically want her just because she wanted him. He'd offered her shelter and comfort when she'd gone a little nuts after Rodney's death, and she wouldn't blame him for that. But obviously a long-term relationship with her wasn't part of his reality.

Did he really believe she'd only wanted a *fling?*

"Shelby…"

"Let's just go."

They left the restaurant, a taut silence stretched between them.

As they entered the hotel, the first person they saw was Oliver Houseman, grinning ear to ear.

"Where have you two been?" He sounded only moderately irritated. "Oh, well, never mind. I have good news. The second the medical examiner took a look at the body, he realized the bullet entered through the neck and out the back of the head. Those imbecile sheriff's deputies don't know an entrance wound from an exit wound."

"Thank God for small favors," Gavin said.

"It's not a small favor, it's a huge one. Everything about the autopsy supports your version of the facts. We've found both of your cars exactly where you said they would be. The woman at the doughnut shop remembers you, Shelby. We have phone records backing up your claim."

"What about the truck?" Gavin asked.

"We haven't found it yet. But the police have ID'd the dead man. His name's Terence Treadwell. An ex-con, served seven years for manslaughter. Paroled in Payton. Ring any bells?"

Shelby struggled to remember such a person, but she came up blank. She shook her head. Gavin did, too. "But it's the third ex-con who's tried to kill me. I bet you'll discover he's a client of Owen's."

At the mention of Owen's name, Oliver frowned. "Yes. About your ex. He's been in court the past two days, all day. Not that he still couldn't have hired someone to do away with you. His connection to the cabin is very suspicious. But he was not the mysterious other person in the truck with Treadwell."

Shelby deflated slightly. She'd been so sure. But when she'd seen Owen, he'd seemed surprised and confused by recent events. If he *was* innocent, it was odd he hadn't remarked about the fact they were so near his fishing cabin. Then again, he'd seemed in a hurry and hadn't asked many questions at all. Perhaps that in itself was suspicious.

"So what's the bottom line?" Gavin asked.

"They're going to drop the charges. Idiots never

should have charged you in the first place," Houseman grumbled.

Shelby was so surprised that for a few moments she just stood there.

"Are we free to go?" Gavin asked.

"Soon as we do a little paperwork."

Gavin felt shell-shocked as he and Shelby boarded a plane later that afternoon. He'd been all geared up for a fight. To suddenly have the problem disappear was almost a letdown.

Not that he wasn't eternally grateful to Oliver Houseman and Ace and even Owen Dorset for the roles they played in setting him and Shelby free. But now his body suffered from a delayed reaction to all that had happened. He was so sore and stiff he could hardly walk, and his mind felt as if it had been numbed with Novocain.

Shelby, too, was unusually quiet. Of course, she'd hardly said three words to him since their discussion at lunch. He knew he'd hurt her feelings. But once she was thinking straight again, once she'd returned to her normal life, she would thank him for not taking advantage of the situation.

With the time difference, it was late by the time they touched down at DFW Airport. They'd been planning to rent a car and drive back to Payton. But as they stepped off the jetway, a crowd started cheering. There were TV cameras, flashbulbs, signs, flags, even a couple of cheerleaders with pom-poms.

"I'm gonna crucify whoever's responsible for this," Shelby said under her breath. Then her face broke into a smile as an older woman came forward, carrying Jake. "Jakey!" Shelby ran and grabbed her son up in her arms.

Then the older woman, whom Gavin guessed was her mother, folded Shelby in a hug. She was swallowed by a crowd of what looked to be friends and family as reporters swarmed around her.

One person in the crowd came forward to greet Gavin—Beau. The two men embraced awkwardly. "Aubrey's waiting in the car. Man, you look like hell."

Been through hell, he wanted to say.

The last glimpse he got of Shelby, she was looking over her shoulder at him, her face full of regret.

Chapter Thirteen

Gavin saw Shelby a couple of days later, when they met at the police station to give Lyle Palmer their story—and their suspicions about Owen. But Shelby and Palmer were already deep in conversation when Gavin arrived, giving him no opportunity to speak privately with Shelby, to try to figure out how to fix things between them.

As the interview progressed, Gavin had to sit on his hands to stop himself from leaping across the desk and strangling Palmer as the detective calmly dismissed their theories. The man was a disgrace to detectives everywhere.

"Frankly, I'm not sure why you want me to pursue this," Lyle said to Shelby, lighting a cigarette in open defiance of the No Smoking ordinance. "This Terence Treadwell was obviously an obsessed nutcase. Just look at his record." Palmer picked up a sheet of paper from his desk and examined it. "He's had three arrests for assaults on women and one conviction for manslaughter for shooting his ex-girlfriend. He was a habitual stalker. Now he's no longer a threat, thanks to Schuyler's fancy gunplay. What's left to investigate?"

"For starters, he was the third ex-con to try to kidnap me in a month's time." Shelby ticked off her points on her elegant fingers, which were properly manicured once again. "Second, I was never Treadwell's girlfriend. His previous acts of violence were against current or former girlfriends. Third, there was another person involved."

"Oh, yes. This second, mysterious person allegedly riding in the truck with Treadwell."

"Allegedly? You think we made him up?"

"I'm sure you thought you saw a second person," Lyle said condescendingly.

Gavin sat harder on his hands. "Someone drove the truck away, and it wasn't Treadwell."

"I'll try to track him down," Lyle said unconvincingly. "But without any leads—"

"How about Treadwell's friends and relatives?" Gavin said in as pleasant a tone as he could manage. "You could start there."

"I know how to conduct an investigation, Schuyler. I don't need your help."

"Apparently you do," Gavin muttered.

"What was that?" Lyle asked sharply.

"Oh, will you two stop it?" Shelby said crossly. With the ordeal a couple of days behind them, she looked much like her old self, wearing a prim turquoise suit, her hair up in its neat twist, a pair of turquoise faux alligator pumps on her feet. But she still had dark circles under her eyes that no amount of makeup could entirely conceal. Though she continued to function normally, the constant fear that she would be assaulted again was apparently taking its toll.

Gavin could only do so much to protect her. He had

a job, and Ace had been tolerant about this whole affair. On his off hours, he tried to keep an eye on her from a distance, and she didn't protest, but she had not recovered her previous warmth toward him. He told himself that once things returned to normal he would get back into her good graces. A romance between them was so unworkable as to be laughable, but he still valued her friendship. However, things would never be normal until they figured out who was trying to kidnap or kill Shelby, and why.

Shelby stood. "Please let me know when you find out something," Shelby said. "And, Detective Palmer, you do know who my father is, right?" She left him with that thought.

Gavin walked with her out of the police department and to her car, ensuring her safety at least that far. "You must be pretty irritated with Palmer to play that card," he said.

"What? What are you talking about?"

"Bringing your father into it. You told me you don't like to rely on family connections."

"I guess when my life is at stake, and the safety of my child, I don't give a flip about my personal ethical standards." She gave him a challenging look, daring him to argue.

Hell, he hadn't meant to start an argument. He'd just been making conversation.

"Shelby, Lyle Palmer isn't going to solve this crime, or this series of crimes. I'm going to investigate myself. I'll take a leave of absence from work if I have to."

Shelby's demeanor changed abruptly. "Oh, Gavin, don't do that. Lyle has warned you not to interfere. What if he arrests you?"

"I can't just do nothing when you're still in danger. I'll try to be discreet, so Palmer doesn't know I'm there."

"Please be careful." She touched his arm, then quickly drew her hand back. He didn't let her escape, though. He caught her hand before she could withdraw entirely.

"Shelby. We need to talk."

"Oh, I think you made yourself very clear." But she didn't snatch her hand away from his hold.

"I may have been wrong. Hell, Shelby, I think maybe I was just trying to make a clean break before things got messy."

"Who says they were going to get messy? I had this notion, and maybe it was naive, that things were going to get better."

They stared at each other, silent, the rate of their breathing in perfect sync, the slight frost of their breaths mingling in the cold air.

"You don't know what you're getting into," Gavin finally said. "Hooking up with someone like me—"

"You mean a person who's decent and honest and hardworking?"

"I mean a guy who has no prospects for the future."

"I don't need some guy to take care of me, to support me and shower me with diamonds. Anyway, given what you've accomplished since you got out of prison, I'd say you have a very bright future."

"What would your family say?"

"They'll like you. After everything you've done to protect me—"

"They like me as your rescuer. They wouldn't like me as your boyfriend."

"Don't underestimate them." She looked as though she wanted to say more, but instead took her hand back, climbed into her car and drove away.

SHELBY TRIED TO FOCUS on her job, on the men and women who depended on her to help them navigate in the real world and stay out of trouble. But her thoughts returned frequently to Gavin. She'd tried to talk herself out of the notion that she might be in love with him. They were, as he'd pointed out, under duress when she'd seduced him on a bed of pine boughs and down jackets. But she was old enough and smart enough to recognize the depth of her own feelings. And now that she was back home, the feelings weren't going away. She wanted him—body and soul—with an intensity that was frightening. And yes, her parents probably would be taken aback if she became involved with an ex-con. And there would be other awkward ramifications to deal with.

She was pleased that Gavin seemed to have had a change of heart. He'd left the door open a crack, anyway. She wouldn't push it, she decided. She would continue to be his friend and let nature take its course.

She saw her latest parolee to the door and was on her way back to her desk when Rosie called to her.

"I need to see you a minute," she said, sounding unusually somber.

Curious, Shelby stepped into Rosie's cubicle, where the morning paper lay on her desk.

"You made some headlines, girl."

"Um, yeah. I saw it earlier." Frankly, she was surprised the media hadn't made a bigger deal of her kidnapping and Gavin's daring rescue, but she was grate-ful they hadn't created too big a fuss. She just wanted things to get back to normal.

"Unfortunately, Ramona read it, too."

"Oh? Why unfortunately?" Shelby sat down, but Rosie seemed too agitated to sit. She fingered her gold lighter, and Shelby could tell she wanted a smoke.

"She remarked to me that Gavin was carrying a gun."

"Yeah, because I made him. Believe me, he didn't want to."

"Still, he shot a man."

"In self-defense. Oh, Rosie, please tell me you aren't going to make something of this. Our lives were at stake. Surely you can see Gavin had no choice but to use that gun."

"I see it, sure. But Ramona—you know what a pain she can be. She said there's been no official ruling on the events in Colorado, and that…well, that I should issue a blue warrant on Gavin."

"Rosie, you can't do that!" A blue warrant would mean Gavin would be locked up again until some de-termination could be made whether he violated parole.

"I don't have any choice. I could lose my job if I don't follow the rules. Anyway, it's just temporary. The facts will exonerate Gavin and they'll let him go. It won't be so bad."

"It'll be terrible. He's trying to live a normal life. He has a job, an apartment, friends. He could lose all that. You'll risk undoing everything he's worked so hard for. Let me talk to Ramona."

"Be my guest. Maybe she'll listen to you. She likes you better than she does me."

But Ramona was a hard-nosed witch, to put it mildly, and she wouldn't back down an inch. She said with the publicity surrounding Gavin, their department would look lax and foolish if they didn't pull him in and at least investigate.

"At least let him come in himself," Shelby pleaded. "Don't have him dragged off in handcuffs."

"He's a flight risk," Ramona said, coolly inspecting her talonlike fingernails.

"No, he's not. I guarantee he's not."

Ramona considered for a minute. "I'll tell Rosie to delay the warrant twenty-four hours. That should give him time to put his affairs in order. And if he comes here voluntarily, we can just walk him over to the jail, nothing flashy. That's the best I can do."

It was better than nothing. "Thanks, Ramona."

"You understand, if he flees, it'll cost you your job."

"Yes, ma'am." But she had faith in Gavin. He wouldn't break the law, even if his freedom was at stake.

GAVIN WORKED FEVERISHLY to locate the white truck. He worked the cases that had piled up on his desk, but whenever there was a lull, he called truck-rental agencies and moving companies—and there were a lot of them.

"Why are you so intent on finding the truck?" Lori asked him. She'd been watching him curiously all morning as she'd gone through her tae kwon do workout. "I mean, the charges have been dropped, haven't they? And the bad guy's dead."

"There are other bad guys out there," Gavin answered. Though the media had portrayed Shelby and him as heroic crime victims who'd fought back, they hadn't told the whole story. "Until I find out who's after Shelby and why, I'm not stopping."

He was also trying to protect himself, though that was a secondary consideration. True, the murder charges had been dropped. But a cloud of suspicion still hung over the improbable story he and Shelby had told. Finding the white truck would go a long way toward verifying the fact they'd been kidnapped.

"Want some help?" Lori asked. "I don't have anything to do."

Gavin smiled gratefully and gave her half the list. He knew she would much rather be out chasing bad guys than stuck on the phone, but until a juicy case walked through the door, she was willing to help. He also gave her Treadwell's mug shot. "We're looking for a plain white truck—"

"I know the routine," Lori assured him. "I've been listening to you all morning, remember?"

By noon, they'd made no progress. Gavin was out of leads and out of ideas. If the truck wasn't a rental, they might never get a lead. And the truck itself might be at the bottom of a lake.

Lori left to pick up some sandwiches for them. Gavin doodled on a legal pad, wondering where he might look next. He could try leaning on the families and associates of all the ex-cons who'd gone after Shelby. But Treadwell's people would never talk to Gavin. And with the others, he risked getting Lyle Palmer all riled up for interfering—if Palmer even found out. Chances were he wouldn't, given the fact he was trying as hard as he could to forget Shelby's case.

The phone rang, and he answered it absently.

"Gavin, I'm glad I caught you." It was Shelby, and a warm rush of pleasure washed over Gavin. Though there was little hope he could ever work things out with Shelby, he couldn't stop his body's physiological reactions to even the sound of her voice.

"What's up? Is everything okay?" He caught the uneasiness in her voice.

"No. Rosie is going to issue a blue warrant on you." She paused, letting that sink in.

And sink in it did. Gavin felt as if the floor was about to cave in beneath him, and he had trouble drawing enough oxygen into his lungs. A blue warrant for parole violation. Arrest. Handcuffs. Jail.

"I explained the circumstances to her, and to Ramona, our supervisor," Shelby continued. "It's not that they don't believe me. But Ramona is a stickler for following the rules. And after the bad publicity following the Manny Cruz and Paulie Sapp incidents, she feels like she has to come down hard."

"That's like closing the barn door after the horses have escaped," Gavin muttered. Damn.

"There will have to be some type of investigation. But all of us feel the facts will exonerate you. So this is only temporary."

"Yeah." Gavin couldn't bring himself to share Shelby's optimism. An investigation could take months, years. Meanwhile he's back in prison, fighting for his survival and his sanity.

"If you come in voluntarily, the matter can be handled quietly. I bought you twenty-four hours. Rosie's expecting you at eleven o'clock tomorrow morning."

"Thank you, Shelby."

There was a long pause. Finally, Shelby said in almost a whisper, "You could get a long way away in twenty-four hours."

Gavin was shocked to the core that Shelby would even think of something like that, much less say it aloud. "You must not think much of my chances for getting out."

She sobbed, the sound clawing at Gavin's heart. "It's not that. I just can't bear the thought of them locking you up again. It's not fair. It shakes my faith in the whole justice system and it makes me want to quit." She paused again, as if weighing her words, pondering what to say next.

Gavin waited patiently, his insides roiling.

"I'd go with you," she blurted out. "Me and Jake. We could go to the Bahamas. My father would help us."

For a moment, Gavin couldn't talk. She was talking about giving up her job, her home, her whole life—for him. Surely she wouldn't go through with something like that. She was just having an emotional reaction, and once she thought it through…

But the fact she would even consider throwing in her lot with him—maybe he'd been too quick to delegitimize her feelings for him.

He and Shelby and Jake and the Bahamas—the temptation was almost too much. The thought of returning to prison made him physically ill—and he might never get out this time. Even if he did, what sort of life could he expect to build afterward? He couldn't expect someone like Ace to come through for him twice in one lifetime.

Gavin let himself visualize a life with Shelby in a tropical paradise. But he only had to consider it a few moments before he realized what a colossal mistake running away would be. Not only would he become a fugitive, he would be turning Shelby into a criminal, as well.

"You're talking nonsense," Gavin said gruffly. "I'll come in tomorrow just like they want. The system isn't perfect, but the facts are on my side. Maybe it will work this time."

"At least let me call in Oliver Houseman."

He wanted to say no. He could never pay Houseman's fees, which meant Shelby would do it—and he wasn't sure his pride could stand that. Then again, they were talking about his freedom, and after seeing Houseman work, he had to conclude the man was far more effective than his old lawyer.

"I'll talk to Houseman," he said, compromising.

"Good. All right." With some effort, she pulled herself together. "Is Lori there, by any chance?"

"She should be back in a few minutes."

"Tell her to call me on my cell. She asked me to look into something for her, and I have some information."

"Does it have to do with her father's murder?"

Shelby sighed. "How did you know about that?"

"Everyone concerned wants her to stay out of it. She might be able to beat up three thugs in a dark alley, but she has no training in investigation. And neither do you, come to think of it. She's liable to get in trouble and drag you with her."

"I'm sure that if she turns up anything interesting, she will take it to the police," Shelby said coolly.

Gavin wasn't so sure. As short a time as he'd known Lori, he knew she liked to think she could handle anything that came her way. "I'll tell her to call."

After hanging up with Shelby, Gavin just sat at his desk, wondering what he should do. He would have to talk to Ace, of course. Maybe put his things in storage. He couldn't be assured he would still have a job or an apartment by the time he got out of jail again.

He hated the thought that he'd be right back where he started.

He thought again about running—without Shelby. He even thought about losing himself in the shimmery oblivion of a drug-induced haze. But in the end, he just opened a new folder and went back to work.

Just as Lori returned with the sandwiches, the phone rang again.

"I'm looking for Gavin Schuyler," a man with a deep, smoker's voice said. Gavin recognized the voice. He'd talked to this man earlier today.

"That would be me."

"You were asking about a white truck? Well, I didn't think that much about it, 'cause all of our trucks are blue. But some cops called from two counties away. They found one of our trucks abandoned on a logging road out in the woods. Someone had painted it white."

Excitement welled up in Gavin's chest. "Can you tell me who rented it?"

"Yeah, but it wasn't either of the fellas you described." Gavin had thought that if Treadwell hadn't rented the truck, Owen Dorset might have, so he'd provided Owen's name and description, as well. "It was a woman."

A woman. Now, that might explain why the truck's mysterious passenger had been so reluctant to help Treadwell.

"Can I come look at the truck?" Gavin asked. One look would tell him whether it was the right truck or not.

"Sure."

"Don't clean it inside or out. Please," he added when he remembered once again that he didn't have police authority behind him.

"No problem."

"Good news?" Lori asked as she spread out their deli sandwiches, chips and drinks on Gavin's desk.

"Possibly. I need to go check it out. So I'll take that sandwich to go." If he could do this one thing during the next twenty-four hours, he might ensure that it wouldn't be his last taste of freedom. "Oh, call Shelby on her cell. She has information for you."

Lori brightened at that news. He left her happily dialing the phone, the receiver tucked under her chin as she took a big bite of her ham-and-Swiss on rye.

Chapter Fourteen

"I finally got around to checking out those names in the ledger book you gave me," Shelby said into the phone.

"There was no rush," Lori said. "I mean, you *have* been a little bit busy escaping from a crazed killer."

The truth was, Shelby had been so distracted after learning of Gavin's impending arrest, she hadn't been able to concentrate at all on her work. She kept thinking about the rash suggestion she'd made, shocked by her own brazen behavior. Was she actually willing to give up the tidy life she'd built in order to live on the lam in another country with Gavin?

She was very afraid she was.

Looking up names on a database had been something easy she could focus on, so she'd dug Lori's ledger book from her purse—she'd never taken it out, and it had survived the whole ordeal to Colorado and back. Then, given what she'd found, she'd become intrigued.

"Three of the names in that book *are* in our computer," Shelby said. "And your father was the judge presiding over all the convictions. Old cases, though. And here's the creepy part. All three are dead."

"Dead, how?"

"One was the victim of prison violence. One killed himself in his cell by tearing up sheets and hanging himself. One died of an accidental drug overdose."

"What kind of criminals were they?"

"Sexual offenders, all. Two were rapists. One a child molester."

"Oh, my God."

"What?"

"Um, nothing. Just that it can't be a coincidence. Maybe the court fines correspond to the amounts in the ledger book?" Lori asked hopefully. "It would make a certain amount of sense, Dad keeping track of the money his rulings had earned."

"No matches—I thought of that. Hey, maybe those amounts are related to restitution. You know, the amount of the fines that went to a victim's assistance program." She hoped, for Lori's sake, that some innocent explanation could be found for the secretive ledger book.

"Maybe," Lori said, not sounding very hopeful. "At least I know where to look now. My father's old cases."

"Lori, be careful." She didn't bother to tell Lori to let the police handle it. They both knew Lyle Palmer would probably do nothing, or at most make a token attempt to check Glenn Bettencourt's old cases.

GAVIN TOOK ONE LOOK at the truck and knew it was the same one. He checked inside. His blood, which had been spread liberally around the truck, had been washed away. But chances were some minute specks remained, if anyone cared to check for them. He examined the rubber bumpers. Shelby's bite marks were clearly there and would be easily matched to her teeth.

Unfortunately, the truck-rental company's owner, one Doug Porter of the smoker's voice, could recall nothing about the woman who rented the truck except that she was neither very young or very old and had dark hair.

"Find what you're looking for?" the gravelly-voiced man asked.

"Sure did."

"Sorry about the cab getting cleaned. By the time I got off the phone with you, our detail man had already gone to work on it. We have to turn our trucks around fast—don't make any money on 'em when they're sitting around in our parking lot, dirty."

"I understand. Could I speak with your detail man?"

"Sure. He's in that first bay over there." The man pointed with his cigarette.

Gavin introduced himself to the man named Steve, whose job it was to vacuum and shampoo the truck's seats and carpets, clean the dash, wash the windows and deodorize the cab. Steve, a short, squat man with an easy smile, seemed anxious to help with a criminal investigation. He somehow got the idea that Gavin was a cop, and Gavin, after correcting him once, gave up trying to set him straight.

"The truck was cleaned out pretty good before I got to it," Steve said. "Not much trash to speak of. But I did find one cigarette butt in the ashtray, stuck way in the back."

That news cheered Gavin up. Cigarette butts were some of the best clues anyone could leave behind. Not only could you match a brand to a suspect, but the butts could contain DNA evidence from saliva. "Do you still have it?"

Steve grinned proudly. "Soon as I heard the truck was involved in a crime, I bagged that cigarette butt up in plastic, just like they do on those cop shows." He showed Gavin his handiwork. The lone cigarette butt was encased in a Ziploc sandwich bag.

Without touching the bag, Gavin visually examined the butt through the plastic. It bore coral-colored lipstick stains, confirming that Treadwell's passenger had been a woman.

"Good work, Steve," Gavin said, patting the man on his shoulder. "In a little while, a detective will come here to collect that bag. I need you to keep it in a safe place."

"I'll lock it in my desk. But can't you take it?"

Gavin wanted to. But if he did, the chain of evidence would be compromised, even if he delivered the butt directly to Lyle Palmer. "Um, a different detective handles the physical evidence," Gavin said vaguely, earning a nod of understanding from Steve.

Back at the office, Gavin took a deep breath and called Lyle Palmer. Palmer was predictably hostile to Gavin's interference, but even he couldn't ignore the fact that Gavin had located the missing truck and some key physical evidence. He grudgingly agreed to have the truck examined by forensics experts.

"I guess I should thank you," Palmer said.

"No thanks necessary. I know how it is on the force— too many cases, not enough manpower." Then he remembered something. "Shelby mentioned that her ex-husband had a new, mysterious girlfriend. Maybe if you could find out who that is…"

"Already on it," Palmer said. He hung up without saying goodbye.

Well, that was that. Nothing left for Gavin to do but get his ducks in a row, then turn himself in.

SHELBY PACED THE LOBBY of the State Building, her newest mauve suede pumps clicking neatly on the dingy tile floor. Some people drank or took drugs or gambled when they were stressed out. Shelby bought shoes. She'd scored three pair last night at the mall.

But even the sale at Saks hadn't cheered her up. Gavin was going back to jail. It was so unfair, so wrong, but she could do nothing to prevent it. In fifteen minutes, he was scheduled to show up in Rosie's cubicle and turn himself in.

She intended to grab him before he got on the elevator and have a private word with him. Some things just had to be said.

He was early. As she watched him pass through the revolving door, silhouetted by the glaring winter sun outdoors, her heart lifted, and only then did she acknowledge the fear she'd harbored that Gavin would flee. Now she knew she needn't have worried. The man Gavin had once been might have run away. But the Gavin she knew, the man she'd fallen in love with, took responsibility for his actions.

"Shelby?" he said in surprise when he realized she was blocking his path to the elevator.

He wore crisp new jeans and a freshly ironed shirt under his jacket. He was also cleanly shaved, his hair recently cut. Hard to believe this was the same scruffy man she'd tromped through the woods with, surviving on energy bars.

"I'm glad you're early," she said. "I wanted a few words with you, away from prying eyes. Will you come with me?"

"Of course."

She'd persuaded the building super to unlock a vacant office on the third floor where their conversation would not be interrupted—or observed. Unfortunately, the office had no furniture. So they stood awkwardly in the middle of the empty space.

"Did you hear I found the truck?" Gavin asked.

"Yes, Lyle called me. I had to go in and identify it, and they took dental impressions so they can match up my bite marks."

"Sounds like for once Lyle is being thorough."

"Yeah."

"And you heard about the cigarette butt?"

"No…what?"

"Treadwell's companion was a woman. She left one lipstick-stained cigarette butt in the ashtray."

Shelby gasped. "Of course. Owen's mysterious girlfriend!"

"Exactly."

Shelby didn't want to waste their scant time together talking about Owen. "Gavin, I have something to tell you."

"Okay." He gazed at her expectantly, those cool green eyes unnerving her. She'd rehearsed what she wanted to say, but now the words wouldn't come easily.

She cleared her throat. "This is going to sound, I

don't know. I don't know what I'm doing. I don't want you to go back to prison."

"It won't be for long," he said. "I had a long talk with Oliver Houseman this morning. He says this is nothing more than a technical glitch. He'll press for an immediate hearing, and he claims he can get me off. As long as you testify."

"Of course I will. Gavin…"

He looked at his watch. She knew he wouldn't risk being late for his appointment with Rosie.

"Gavin, I love you. There, I've said it. I don't care about your past, I don't care about your prospects. I know you're a good man, and that's all that matters to me."

Gavin swallowed. "You can't love me."

"Don't tell me whom I can and can't love! I pick you. What's more, I know you have feelings for me."

"Of course I do!" He turned away from her, walked to the windows and looked out onto the busy downtown street. "How could I not? You're everything that's good and decent and beautiful."

"Then what's the problem?"

"I won't take you down with me."

She joined him at the window, slipped her arm around his waist, inside his jacket. His skin felt hot beneath the starchy cotton of his shirt. "You're not going down. You're suffering a temporary setback."

"Maybe. Or maybe Houseman's blowing hot air. But even if I do get out—good Lord, Shelby, you can do better than me."

"I don't think so," she said evenly. "I love you, you're stuck with it. You can turn me away if you really want to, if you don't want to be with me. But I won't let you deny what's between us out of some misguided attempt to protect me."

"Owen would never let you associate with an ex-con. He would take Jake away from you."

She'd thought of that, and the possibility of losing custody of Jake had given her pause. "Owen's going to be in jail."

"We hope. But what if he isn't? What if we just can't come up with enough evidence? Or what if he's not involved after all?"

"Let me worry about Owen. Stick with the issue. I love you, and I'm going to keep on loving you. What are you going to do about it?"

He stared at her for several heartbeats, and she thought he was going to kiss her. She could get through what came next, if only he would kiss her. But he didn't. He turned away and headed for the door.

"I'm going to wait for you to get over it," he said over his shoulder. "Face it, Shelby, you've got a bad-boy complex. Find a nice, safe accountant to fall in love with." And he left.

Shelby just stood there, stunned. She'd played the ace up her sleeve, but she'd lost the game anyway.

Did she have a bad-boy complex? Maybe she did find dark and dangerous men somewhat intriguing, but that wasn't what she'd fallen in love with. She'd fallen for Gavin's kindness. His protectiveness. His honor. His work ethic, and his willingness to accept responsibility for his actions. His determination to change his life for the better. These weren't bad-boy qualities.

But he wasn't going to believe her, no matter what

she said. He was *still* trying to protect her from what he perceived to be her own foolish choices.

She couldn't help herself. She kicked the wall, putting a big scuff on her suede shoe. Then, feeling stupid, she sank to the floor, massaged her throbbing toe and wondered how she was going to live the rest of her life without Gavin Schuyler.

GAVIN HAD TO FORCE HIMSELF to put one foot in front of the other as he entered the parole office. He passed through a metal detector—newly installed since Shelby's unfortunate encounter with Manny Cruz—and told the receptionist he was reporting to Rosie Amadeo.

Rosie came up front to meet him, smiling tentatively. "You made it. Five minutes early, too."

"You expected me not to?"

"No, I knew you'd be here. Let's go back to my office. I have some paperwork to finish. Then a guard from county lockup across the street will walk you over."

"The county jail?" Gavin asked, surprised, as they made their way through the rabbit warren of cubicles toward Rosie's station. "I'm not going back to Huntsville?"

"Not for now. Due to the mitigating circumstances, we're hoping to get a hearing scheduled within a couple of weeks. No sense processing you into Huntsville for such a short time."

This sounded promising. Apparently Rosie believed his parole revocation was only temporary. Suddenly he felt a bit more kindly toward Rosie than he had before.

"I appreciate how you've handled this," he said as he

sat down in the chair across from her desk. Her cubicle was a bit smaller than Shelby's, the furniture not as nice.

"I wish we didn't have to do it at all. But sometimes we just have to follow the rules, even if they don't make sense. This will only take a few minutes. Have some M&M's."

She swiveled her chair toward her computer on the credenza and began typing, rapid-fire. Gavin didn't understand how she typed so fast with those two-inch nails.

He helped himself to a handful of peanut M&M's. Then, something on Rosie's desk snagged his attention. She'd left an open pack of cigarettes there, as if maybe she'd just returned from a smoke break. Peeking out the top of the pack was a half-smoked butt—and those lipstick stains looked mighty familiar.

He tried to tell himself it was just a coincidence. But then he started to think about it. Shelby had been on her way to help Rosie move into her new apartment and had offered to stop and get doughnuts. Rosie knew where she would be, and could have sent Treadwell there to ambush her.

But Rosie was Shelby's best friend, wasn't she?

Gavin wasn't taking any chances. With Rosie's attention firmly on her computer, she wasn't watching him. He slid the partially smoked cigarette out of the pack, palmed it and slid it into the top of his boot.

Rosie's printer started humming, and a document spewed out of it. At the same time, her phone rang. She answered it, listened, said "un-huh" a couple of times, then hung up.

She smiled brightly and stood. "That's our cue." She snatched up the document from her printer and led Gavin away.

SHELBY MADE IT THROUGH the day somehow. She met with her clients, listened, took notes, offered advice. When one man didn't show up for his appointment, she called his house and got his wife, who said he was too drunk to come in. Reluctantly she issued a blue warrant, thinking longer and harder about the effect such an action would have on his wife, his kids. But she'd given this one all the leeway she could.

By the end of the day she was more than ready to go home. She avoided Rosie—an encounter with her would inevitably lead to a conversation about sending Gavin back to jail, and she wasn't up to it. She didn't want anyone to know how profoundly this whole thing had messed her up.

She was surprised to discover Oliver Houseman waiting at her car. She offered him a warm smile. He was one of the few true allies Gavin had, and she was grateful for everything he'd done for them. She'd assured him she would be responsible for any fees associated with Gavin's defense.

"You don't clock out at five, do you?" she asked, assuming he wanted to interview her further about the circumstances surrounding Gavin's purported parole violation. He was nothing if not thorough.

"Actually, I am off the clock," Houseman said. "I'm here to deliver a strictly personal message from Gavin."

She frowned and leaned against her Volvo without unlocking the door. "Don't tell me. He wants you to make sure I understand he rejected me for my own good. Right?"

Houseman looked confused. "No, actually. Gavin has come up with a suspect for the mysterious truck passenger. It's someone you know, and he wanted to warn you about her."

"What? Who?"

"Rosie Amadeo. Someone you work with, I take it?"

At first, Shelby thought she hadn't heard right. "Rosie?" she said on a laugh. "He thinks Rosie had something to do with the assaults and kidnappings? Oh, my gosh, he's lost it. Rosie is my best friend. Why would he think something so crazy?"

"You know he collected a cigarette butt with a lipstick stain from the truck, right?"

"Yeah, so? Oh, of course. Rosie smokes and wears lipstick. For heaven's sake, millions of women smoke and wear lipstick." She was ranting now. But the day's pressures had gotten to her.

Houseman remained completely unruffled in the face of her emotional reaction. "It was her brand of smokes," he said with a shrug. "He says he'll know for sure in a few days. Meanwhile, he just wants you to be very careful."

Shelby just shook her head. "I am always very careful, Mr. Houseman. But Gavin has gone way over the top here. I know he's desperate to redeem himself by catching my would-be killer, but he's grasping at straws."

Houseman shrugged again. "I'm just the messenger boy."

She shook his hand. "Thank you. You can tell Gavin his warning has been duly noted." No need to distress Gavin further by telling him she thought he was nuts to suspect her best friend.

Shelby picked up Jake from day care—just seeing his cheerful little face made her feel better. Then she stopped at the grocery store to buy the ingredients for one of her favorite guilty pleasures. She was going to bake a big ol' Frito-chili pie and wash it down with cheap wine. Rosie was coming over for dinner, and Shelby intended to indulge in fat grams, alcohol and a heavy dose of girl talk. She needed to confide in someone.

She would not, however, reveal Gavin's suspicions. She knew once she said the words aloud, she and Rosie would start laughing hysterically at the notion that Rosie would want to harm Shelby in any way. And she did not want to laugh at Gavin's expense.

Rosie showed up at Shelby's condo just as Shelby was taking the Frito pie out of the oven.

"Oh, my gosh, I can smell it from the door," she said as she entered without knocking.

Shelby smiled at her friend, smiled even bigger when she saw the three-layer chocolate cake Rosie carried. "Courtesy of my mom," Rosie said as she set the cake down on Shelby's breakfast bar. "Ever since I moved to my own place, she's been cooking and baking for me constantly. My freezer and fridge are packed."

"Maybe we should have had dinner at your house," Shelby said as she opened the wine. "The casserole needs to cool a few minutes. Want to go sit out on the sunporch?"

"I'll get the wineglasses."

The sunporch was their favorite place to sit, drink wine and ponder life's mysteries. With the ceiling fan on and a couple of windows open a crack, Rosie could smoke and the pattern of air circulation would blow the smoke right outside.

But Rosie didn't light up. Instead, she pulled Jake

into her lap. "How're you doin', big guy? Hey, isn't he supposed to be with Owen this week?"

"Owen's been uncharacteristically generous since my ordeal in Colorado. He insisted I keep Jake this week, to make up for the time I missed."

"There now, see, Owen's not so bad sometimes."

"Sometimes." Or maybe he was feeling guilty for trying to have her killed. Lyle had told her Owen was still considered a suspect. But until they had more evidence against him, they couldn't move. Apparently the fact the kidnapper used Owen's cabin wasn't enough, since virtually anyone could have known Owen owned the cabin. He'd taken dozens of friends and associates up there, and Shelby herself had mentioned it to scores of people over the years.

Rosie sighed. "Kids are just so cute at this age. If my baby had lived, she would be over a year old now. Walking, talking…"

Shelby never knew what to say when Rosie brought up this subject. To reassure her that she would have more children seemed trite. So she took a sip of her wine. "Ugh, maybe I should invest a few more bucks in the wine next time. This is pretty vile."

"It'll get better by the second glass," Rosie said with a laugh, and the tension passed. They talked about work and silly, girlie things like which moisturizer they liked best and what they were getting Leslie, one of their co-workers, as a wedding gift. It was soothing, and Shelby decided she didn't want to talk about Gavin to Rosie. It was too painful, too personal. She needed more time to process the fact that there wasn't going to be a happily-ever-after for them.

Shelby reached for her wineglass, intending to refill it, but it was full. "Oh, a magic wineglass," she said with a smile.

"I don't want to be the only one getting snockered. Cheers." Rosie lifted her glass in a toast, and Shelby joined her. The wine didn't taste any better on the second glass, but she drank it anyway.

As they left the porch and headed for the kitchen, ready to dish up the Frito pie, Shelby's phone rang. She answered the kitchen extension as she cut the casserole, figuring it was a telemarketer. They always managed to call just as she sat down to dinner.

"Shelby, it's Gavin."

She nearly dropped her spatula. "Um, hi." Rosie was setting the table in the dining room, out of earshot. "How—how are you?" Lame, Shelby. But she was so surprised. She had a million things she wanted to say. She was still angry with him for dismissing her love, and for suspecting dear, funny Rosie. But no angry words came to her lips. In fact, she felt a little fuzzy around the edges.

"Listen, I don't have much time. Did Oliver Houseman talk to you about Rosie?"

"Yes. And it's the most ridiculous—"

"Listen to me," he said, cutting her off with uncharacteristic rudeness. "Craig sent the cigarette butt to the lab—the one from the truck, and the one I snitched from Rosie's desk. They match."

"I don't believe it. You—you couldn't possibly get lab results back that fast."

"Craig personally delivered the evidence to a friend, who examined the lip prints with a comparison microscope. They're doing a DNA comparison now, and that will take time. But once they have that, they'll be arresting Rosie. I want you to promise me you'll steer clear of her."

Shelby's head was spinning. "How could it be true?" But why would Gavin lie about this? He wouldn't. "It must be a mistake of some kind. She has no reason…"

Rosie had returned to the kitchen to get napkins, utterly unaware of the life-altering conversation taking place. And suddenly it all made sense.

She recalled Rosie, urging her to take a vacation; Rosie, who had access to Shelby's credit card and personal information; Rosie, who placed Shelby in the store parking lot where she was kidnapped; Rosie, quietly envious of Shelby's money, her clothes, her healthy child. Rosie, her best friend—and Owen's secret girlfriend.

"Shelby?" Gavin asked. "You okay?"

At the same time, Rosie was looking at her, concerned. "Hey, you okay? Who is that?"

No, she wasn't okay. Her head was spinning like a merry-go-round, and she felt as if she wanted to throw up.

"It's, um, it's nobody. An obscene caller."

Rosie rolled her eyes. "Honey, just hang up."

Shelby did. She didn't want Rosie to know Gavin had called. She didn't want Rosie to know she'd been tipped off. She just wanted to get Rosie out of her house, away from her and away from her child.

"You know, I don't feel too hot."

"You're probably just hungry. You never eat enough." She led Shelby to the dining room and sat her down. Moments later she set a full plate in front of Shelby—and a full wineglass. "Eat," she commanded. Then she watched intently to make certain Shelby followed orders.

"The wine," Shelby murmured. She looked up at her friend and saw someone she'd never seen before. "You poisoned the wine."

Rosie's eyes widened. "What?"

"Nothing." Shelby struggled to clear her head enough that she could figure out what to do. "Oh, I forgot the salt." She stood and headed for the kitchen, intending to grab the phone and dial 9-1-1. But she didn't get far.

"Shelby."

Shelby focused her eyes on Rosie, who held Jake in her arms—and had a gun pointed at him.

Chapter Fifteen

Gavin stared at the phone receiver. What had that been about? Why had Shelby hung up on him? It hadn't sounded as though she was angry. She'd sounded distant, sort of disoriented. She'd said something about an obscene phone call, but her voice had been muffled, as if she'd been talking to…someone else.

Oh, God. Rosie was with her at that very moment. Every instinct Gavin possessed told him Shelby was in trouble.

The sheriff's deputy who'd allowed him to use the phone—an old buddy from the police academy, one Bryson Kelly—now took the receiver from Gavin's hand and hung it up.

"Wait, I need to make another call."

"Have a heart, Schuyler. I'm breaking at least ten rules by letting you use the phone. I need to get you back to your cell before Ruthie gets back from dinner."

Ruthie Collier was the other deputy assigned guard duty that night at the tiny, low-security county lockup. Gavin was still amazed they'd let him stay here. But since everyone seemed to think next week's hearing would exonerate him, they didn't consider him a flight risk. But low security or not, the guard named Ruthie would have kittens if she caught Gavin out of his cell.

He understood Bryson's unease. But Shelby's life was at risk.

"Listen, Bryce, just one more quick call. It could be a matter of life and death."

"That's what they all say." A noise at the outer door caused a look of panic to come into Bryson's eyes. He grabbed Gavin's arm and attempted to drag him back to his cell. "For God's sake, you want me to lose my job?"

Gavin hated what he was about to do, because he was about to ensure that he spent the next dozen or so years behind bars. But he could not sit by while Shelby was at a killer's mercy. Something was very wrong at her house. And it would waste precious minutes if he tried to explain the situation to Bryce.

"I'm sorry, Bryce." He coldcocked the guard, who crumpled to the ground unconscious. He reached for Bryson's gun, then decided against it. If he had a gun, it would be much easier for some hotshot cop to shoot him dead.

Anyway, he had no desire to use deadly force.

He met Ruthie, a stout, boxy woman with frizzled blond hair, as she came through the door loaded down with fast-food bags.

She took one look at Gavin, dropped the food and drinks, and backed up against the wall.

"Holy Christ!"

Gavin didn't wait for her to pull herself together and draw her weapon. He darted out the door and into the anonymity of winter darkness. In moments he'd cleared a chain-link fence, cut through a parking lot, then over a wall into an apartment complex. He heard shouts and sirens behind him, which would bring people out of their apartments or peeking through curtains to see what the problem was. Anyone who saw a man running would be immediately suspicious. He screeched to a halt, walking slowly, looking around as if he, too, was curious about the sirens.

A woman opened her front door as he walked past. He gave her a friendly wave. "Sounds like something's going on at the jail."

"I swear, they can't keep people locked up at that place. This is the third escape this year." She returned inside and closed her door.

Gavin breathed a sigh of relief. He needed a phone and transportation, in that order. What he found was a bicycle—miraculously unlocked. He grabbed it, hopped on and pedaled out of the parking lot. The tires were almost flat, but it would get him out of the immediate area.

He zigzagged through a residential neighborhood, disoriented for a few moments until he came out into the parking lot of a seedy shopping area and realized he was only a few blocks from First Strike.

Time was slipping away, but his initial panic over Shelby's fate had been pushed to the wayside by cool logic. If he was going to save her life, he had to think clearly and behave logically.

He rode by the office first, hoping someone might be there after hours. But the office was dark. However, Taft Bail Bonds was open twenty-four hours, and Benny Taft knew him. Gavin dropped the bike to the sidewalk and slid inside the bondsman's office.

Benny's wife, Antonette, was working the front desk. She looked startled to see him, raising both severely plucked eyebrows. "Thought you were in the clink."

"Antonette, I need your phone. It's an emergency."

As if sensing Gavin's carefully banked desperation, Antonette swiveled her phone around and handed him the receiver.

Gavin dialed Ace's number and thankfully found him at home. "Listen, I need you to round up Beau and Rex and Lori and meet me at the office. I know who's been trying to kill Shelby, and she's in danger as we speak."

"Gavin? Where are you?"

"Please, Ace, trust me this one last time."

"You got it. I'll be there with the cavalry as fast as I can."

"Rosie, why?" was all Shelby could think of to say.

"You have to ask?" Rosie's face twisted with hatred. "You're even stupider than I thought."

"Please, don't hurt my baby. What do you want from me?"

"That should be obvious. I want you dead."

"But why? You've got Owen. I would never stand in the way of you two. I have no feelings left for him, and he certainly is over me."

"Then why did he jump out of bed and fly to Colorado the moment your father called him? Because poor Shelby needed him. It's all Owen ever wanted, to be needed, looked up to, admired. But you were so busy with your career and your causes and your child."

"If Owen hurried to help me, it was because he thought he could grab some headlines," Shelby said.

"He doesn't care anything about me. Put the gun down, Rosie. You need help. Let me get you some help."

"Let you put me behind bars, you mean. No, thanks. We both know I'm in it too deep now to get off with counseling. Damn it, if only that stupid Manny had gone through with the job. And Paulie—jeez, could anything get more fouled up than that? And Treadwell—he was supposed to be a professional. You're like a cat with nine lives. But I guess if you want a job done right, you have to do it yourself."

"I could make you use that gun," Shelby said. "You'd never get away with it then."

"Who says? The gun's not traceable. I could claim an intruder broke in while we were having dinner. But I won't have to use the gun. You don't have the guts to do anything dangerous, not when I'm holding your child."

"You wouldn't hurt Jake."

"You're right, I wouldn't kill him," Rosie said coolly, though she continued to point the gun at Jake's head. "He's going to be *my* child, after all, the child I was supposed to have. And I'm going to have the perfect family—me, Owen and Jakey. The family you threw away."

"You could have had all that without killing me," Shelby said, wanting to understand.

"I didn't want a part-time child. Or a husband who saw his ex-wife twice a week and still had her phone number on his speed dial. Anyway, I couldn't get the money without getting rid of you."

"What money?"

"The life insurance. A quarter of a million bucks. Half a million, if it's ruled an accident. I found the policy in Owen's file cabinet. I love Owen, but let's face it, his law practice isn't exactly a big moneymaker. I want everything you had—your family, your money, your freaking shoes. You've always had everything handed to you. Your daddy is the governor's golfing buddy, and everybody knows it, and everybody gives you what you want. Even Ramona. And I get crumbs, because my father's dead and my mother was a maid, and I couldn't even have a baby right and my husband walked out."

Life insurance. So that's what this was all about? Shelby debated whether to tell Rosie the policy had been canceled long ago—she'd checked. She decided not to—it might tip Rosie over the edge.

Jake had started to cry, and the sound tore at Shelby. She wanted to rush Rosie, to snatch her child out of that monster's arms. But her legs wouldn't obey her brain. Whatever drug had been in the wine was doing its job, now.

"What did you put in the wine?"

"Succinylcholine," Rosie said with a triumphant smile. "Eventually it will paralyze your respiratory system and you'll suffocate. And it won't show up on a routine drug screen."

"Sounds like you've done your research." Shelby didn't know if it was merely the power of suggestion, but she was finding it hard to breathe. And she still couldn't get her arms and legs to cooperate. She sank onto the floor, hardly remembering how she got there.

A noise at the front door jerked Rosie's attention away from Shelby. Shelby wanted to cry out, to warn whoever was there not to burst in, for fear Rosie would panic and pull the trigger. But no words would form.

Dark clouds encroached around the edge of her vision. Yet she was still perfectly aware of what was going on around her.

The door opened—she probably hadn't locked it after letting Rosie in.

"Oh, my God."

It was Owen. Poor Owen, Shelby's number-one suspect, blissfully ignorant that his hot new girlfriend was a homicidal maniac.

"Just back out, Owen. Just leave. I'm doing this for us, don't you understand? We won't have to share Jake anymore. And the insurance money—we could buy any house we want. Any cars we want. So just get out, and pretend you never saw any of this."

Would he? Shelby wondered.

But no, he didn't. He was kneeling beside her, taking her pulse, looking into her eyes. "What'd you do to her?" he asked Rosie desperately.

"She's in no pain. She'll be gone in a few minutes." Owen stood. "I'm calling for an ambulance."

"Don't you do it. Don't you reach for that phone—"

Shelby couldn't see what was going on. But then the blast of the gun blotted out everything else. Oh, God. Had she been shot? Had Owen? Jakey? Had Rosie taken her own life? She wanted to turn her head, but she couldn't. All she could see was the ceiling.

"Change of plans," Rosie said quietly. Jake's cries had grown frantic. Thank God, he was still alive. "Murder-suicide makes perfect sense."

FIVE BOUNTY HUNTERS and all of their equipment were a tight fit in Rex's black Bronco. When they reached the block where Shelby's condo was located, they stopped a few doors down and piled out, donning Kevlar vests and loading guns as they moved.

"There's a back door that leads through a sunporch and into a courtyard," said Lori, the only one of them to actually visit Shelby's home.

"No garage?" Rex asked, scanning the trendy condo complex, where the units were all shaped like vertical Ls.

"No. She has a detached garage somewhere behind the complex. Other possible access points are windows front and back, both floors. She also has a skylight in the kitchen, where it's only one floor."

"Anyone know who these cars belong to?" Ace asked of the two vehicles parallel parked at the curb.

"The BMW is Owen's," Gavin said grimly. He'd made it his business to learn everything he could about Shelby's ex. It looked as if perhaps he and Rosie were in this together.

"Gavin, it's your call," Ace said. "How do you want to proceed?"

Gavin didn't hesitate. "Ace and Lori, I want you at the back door." He knew Ace would direct Lori's actions and protect her. "Rex and Beau, take the front. We move together, on my signal."

Everyone checked that their two-way headset radios were working, then moved quickly and quietly to their assigned positions. Gavin climbed a live oak tree, giving him access to the first-story roof. He located the skylight, but it was frosted glass—impossible to see inside.

"Anyone got a visual?"

"There are people inside," Beau reported. "I can see through a crack in the blinds. I see a woman with dark hair standing with her back to me. She's holding a child."

"A couple of windows are open to the sunporch," Ace said. "We can get in easy."

"Do it," Gavin said. "The dark-haired woman is our perp. If there's a man in there with her, he could be dangerous, too. They'll undoubtedly use the child to gain Shelby's cooperation."

"We're inside," Ace said quietly. "The door into the kitchen is locked, but I've got a clear view through a window and into the dining room. I see the woman, too. She's—oh, holy hell, she's got a gun."

Gavin hesitated a fraction of a second. He wanted more than anything to just burst in, to wrest the gun away from Rosie, to pull Shelby and Jake out and get them to safety. But only a hothead bounty hunter would resort to such action.

"We should let her know we're here," Gavin said. "Try to talk to—" The sound of gunfire cut off what he was about to say. "Never mind. Let's move—now." Using a tool designed to break out car windows, Gavin shattered the skylight. "Police!" he yelled, a purely instinctual thing. Hell, what did it matter if he added impersonating a police officer to his list of charges? He was going away for a long, long time no matter what.

He dropped down through the skylight just as Ace kicked in the kitchen door, and the three of them converged in the kitchen. Gavin's leg twinged with pain when he hit the floor, but it held strong.

Gavin nodded toward the dining room. They heard Rex and Beau coming through the front door, yelling "Freeze" and "Drop your weapon!"

Gavin peered around the corner into the dining room, then froze as he saw two bodies on the floor. One of them was Owen Dorset, with a hole in his chest big enough to drive a tank through. The other was Shelby, splattered with blood, still as a marble statue.

"Oh, God, no."

"Stop right there. I'll kill this baby."

Gavin didn't move a muscle. He darted a look at Rosie, who held a screaming Jake in a death grip, her impossibly huge gun pointed straight at the child's head. Then he looked back at Shelby. Her eyes flickered with life. He had to save her. He had to, or all of this had been in vain.

"Rosie, you will not harm a child," Gavin said. "I know you, not just from our contact, but from what Shelby has said about you. You love children. You would never harm an innocent child."

Rosie stared at him, surprised. "Why aren't you in jail?"

"They let me out," he lied. "Because they know now who the real culprit is. You left a cigarette butt in the truck's ashtray. Lab tests proved it was yours. The police know everything, Rosie. It's over. And unless you want to face the death penalty, you'll drop the gun and hand over the child."

"It's not over. You think you and your pathetic little band of ex-cons and ex-cops, failures who couldn't make it in legitimate law enforcement, are going to take me in? Not while I've got Jake. You're all going to drop your weapons, and I'm going to walk out of here, get in my car and drive away. It's the only way you'll get

Shelby help in time to save her life. Otherwise, she's just going to suffocate right here in front of you."

"Shelby would rather die than let you walk away with her son, Rosie," Gavin said. He laid down his gun, stepped forward and held out his arms. "Give him to me. Don't make us kill you. There's been too much blood-shed already."

He stepped closer. Rosie stepped back. God, he hoped he was right, that Rosie wouldn't kill Jake. But if he understood her at all, she killed only when she felt it was justified. She killed only those who threatened her, or who got between her and her goals. Jake was a complete innocent. And she still had enough humanity in her to recognize that.

That was one thing he'd learned in prison. Every criminal, no matter how depraved, had some type of moral compass, even if it was radically skewed.

He stepped closer, only inches from her now. "It's over now, Rosie. Give me Jake. Save your own life."

"I'm not going to jail."

"Maybe you won't have to. You didn't actually mur-der anyone, did you?" Never mind her lover's body lying inert on the floor. "Anyone could understand. You were provoked beyond reason. You were justified. You were only trying to protect yourself."

Tears coursed down Rosie's cheeks, leaving black rivulets of smeared mascara. "Yes, that's right."

"There's still a way out, Rosie. Give me Jake." He came closer. He was actually touching the boy now. Jake squalled and reached out his arms toward Gavin. Gavin clamped his hands onto Jake's sturdy little body and tugged. "It's real easy. Just loosen your hold."

Miraculously, she did.

"That's it." Jake was in his arms now. Gavin slowly turned, shielding Jake from the reach of Rosie's weapon, and stepped away. It was up to the others to finish the job he'd started.

He heard a thump—then four bounty hunters leaped into action, dragging Rosie to the ground and cuffing her.

Gavin didn't spare a moment of attention to the action taking place behind him. He dropped to Shelby's side, setting Jake down on the carpet beside him.

"Shelby? Honey, where are you hurt?"

Her eyes fluttered closed. He realized she wasn't breathing and immediately began CPR, clamping his mouth over hers not in passion, but desperation.

Beau lent his efforts, pumping Shelby's heart while Gavin filled her lungs over and over. *C'mon, honey, breathe.* But she wouldn't breathe on her own. They kept at it as sirens approached, moving away from Shelby only when paramedics arrived and took over.

"Poison, do you think?" Ace asked.

"Perp has some kind of powder in her pocket," said one of the uniforms who'd taken custody of Rosie.

Gavin turned back to Rosie. "What is it?" he demanded.

"Cooperate now, and it'll help you down the road."

"It's succinylcholine," Rosie said sullenly. "Get her on a respirator. She might live. Or she might not."

Gavin turned, intending to report this information to the paramedics. He ran smack into Lyle Palmer.

"Thought I might find you here," Palmer said smugly. "You're a piece of work."

"I'll talk to the paramedics," said Lori, who'd heard Rosie's information about the poison.

Gavin realized he could do nothing more. He held out his hands, passively accepting the handcuffs one of the uniforms clasped around his wrists.

Chapter Sixteen

"They're going to lock me up and throw away the key," Gavin muttered miserably as two guards helped him out of the prison van. He was shackled hand and foot, back wearing the hated orange prison jumpsuit. Oliver Houseman had tried everything, but they weren't even allowing Gavin to wear street clothes, or appear without shackles.

After his last escapade, he supposed he didn't blame them.

Today's hearing was before the parole board, which would decide whether to revoke his parole. Gavin wasn't sure why Houseman was even bothering to put up an argument. Seemed like a slam-dunk decision to him.

When he'd made his daring escape from the county jail, he'd told himself he would gladly suffer any consequences, if only he could save Shelby's life. If he could do that one thing, he would know in his heart that his life had been worth living, and that knowledge would make incarceration bearable.

Well, Shelby had lived. They had put her on a respirator, and things had looked grim for a few hours. But the drug Rosie had used to poison Shelby had gradually worked its way out of her system, and within a few hours she'd been breathing on her own again. She'd suffered no permanent ill effects from her brush with death.

Unfortunately, Owen wasn't so lucky.

Gavin had heard all this secondhand, from his lawyer. He hadn't been allowed any other visitors.

The only direct communication he'd had from Shelby was a letter, short and to the point, the contents of which he'd memorized. *I love you. I will wait for you forever.*

Sentimental nonsense, he told himself, probably written before her senses had returned to normal. Sooner or later, he would be allowed to see her face-to-face. When he did, he would straighten her out. He could live with the things he'd done, the decisions he'd made. He could not live with the knowledge that the finest woman he'd ever known was wasting the best years of her life, waiting for a man who might spend the next twenty or thirty years behind bars.

Meanwhile, though, he couldn't help but cherish her words. If a woman like Shelby could love him, there was hope for him yet.

Several reporters and photographers attempted to intercept him as the guards escorted him into the county courthouse. He did not duck his head or cover his face, as if he were ashamed. Neither did he smile, or answer any of the inflammatory questions the reporters hurled his way. He just looked straight ahead, wishing the ordeal was over with.

As he entered the courtroom, which was crowded with more media and curious onlookers, he scanned the room for Shelby. When he found her, looking serious in a navy suit, his heart lifted even as it ached with longing.

She'd been watching for him, too. Their eyes met, and she managed a watery smile and a thumbs-up. Though Houseman had reassured him she was fine, he was relieved to see for himself that she was walking, talking, breathing. He took his seat next to Houseman.

This parole hearing was nothing like his last one, which had been quick and informal. It felt much more like a criminal trial, as prison officials and prosecutors presented their long list of grievances against him, everything from killing a man to stealing a bicycle, making him sound like a hardened criminal with no hope of being rehabilitated.

Having Bryson Kelly take the stand, his face still bruised purple from where Gavin had socked him, didn't help his case any, although the guard did mention that Gavin could have taken his gun but chose not to.

Their star witness was none other than Detective Lyle Palmer, who achieved just the right note of righteous indignation and regret over one of their own gone bad.

Someday he was going to get that bastard. He'd seen Lyle pocket cash during a drug bust, and that was only the tip of the corruption iceberg. But at the time of Gavin's arrest, his lawyer hadn't thought it would help Gavin to muddy the waters by throwing out accusations of others' guilt.

Gavin was afraid to even look at the parole-board officials, who no doubt sported grim mouths and accusing stares. Hell, he'd put *himself* away if he'd had to make a decision based on what he'd just heard.

Then Houseman got his shot. He had a list of witnesses long enough to paper the whole courtroom, starting with a police official from Blair County, Colorado, who stated that there was no indication the shooting in the woods had been anything other than self-defense.

Next he brought in local police officials who were willing to go on the record saying Shelby would have died had Gavin not taken the action he did. He even brought on the owner of the stolen bicycle, who testified that before he'd been taken to jail, he'd asked one of the uniforms to return the bike to its lawful owner.

Last to speak was Shelby herself, detailing Gavin's repeated attempts to protect her, his initial refusal to even touch Treadwell's gun, his willingness to turn himself in when he could have fled. Unfortunately, her testimony lost some of its punch when one of the parole officials questioned her as to her romantic involvement with Gavin. She flushed bright pink as she admitted that she had very strong feelings for Gavin, and that they'd become physically intimate during their ordeal on the mountain.

"That hurt," Houseman whispered.

Unlike a criminal trial, which might have gone on for days or weeks, the hearing took only one day. At 4 p.m., the parole-board members retired to deliberate. They took less than an hour. Their spokesman, an older woman with iron-gray hair and a face that hardly moved, delivered their decision.

"This is a complex case, and I'm afraid there is no one right or fair way to make a ruling," she began. Gavin didn't think this sounded good. "Mr. Schuyler has some devoted fans," she continued, "and we recognize that his intentions, when breaking the rules of his parole, were wholly honorable. Therefore we would not revoke his parole based on the incident in Colorado. However—" she hurried on, lest anyone get the wrong idea "—breaking out of jail, assaulting guards and theft of property are not parole violations. These are crimes. Yes, there were powerful extenuating circumstances, but it's not our place to determine Mr. Schuyler's guilt or innocence. Therefore, it is this board's recommendation that Mr. Schuyler be placed in custody and held without bond until the new charges against him can be satisfied."

As the courtroom broke out in an excited buzz, Houseman leaned over and murmured, "We haven't lost yet. We'll keep fighting."

Gavin appreciated Houseman's spirit, but he suspected the lawyer would keep fighting more to keep his name in the paper than out of any real belief Gavin would go free. Gavin had no illusions that he would be found innocent. No one could argue that he hadn't committed those crimes. And Texas juries were notoriously hardhearted about repeat offenders, whatever the mitigating circumstances. He might be looking at serving his entire ten-year sentence, plus more for the new crimes.

He chanced a look at Shelby. Her cheeks were wet with tears, which she made no attempt to wipe away. The sight of her pain just about did him in.

Gavin stood, preparing to be led out the back door to the waiting prison van. Suddenly the door at the back burst open, and a group of important-looking men and women strode into the courtroom. Leading the way was an older man Gavin thought looked familiar. He had snow-white, curly hair and a matching handlebar mustache, and he wore a bolo tie.

"Holy crap," the usually unflappable Oliver House-man said. Everyone else fell into a frozen silence as the important-looking man and his entourage made their way to the front of the courtroom.

"Did I miss the whole thing?" the man asked.

The gray-haired woman from the parole board stepped forward. "Governor Wilson. Yes, sir, we just finished up."

"And are you sending the young man—confound it, what's his name?"

"Schuyler," answered a young woman standing at his elbow. "Gavin Schuyler."

"Yes. Are you sending him back to jail?"

"Yes, sir, pending the outcome of the charges recently filed—"

"Well, let him go. Are you people out of your minds? He saved my goddaughter's life, not once, but on multiple occasions. He's not a criminal, he's a hero!"

The governor's voice boomed through the courtroom. After he spoke, there was such a profound silence, the room could have been empty. Gavin scarcely breathed.

The governor of Texas was standing not twenty feet from him, demanding that he be freed. And he knew who was responsible. Shelby, the governor's goddaughter, apparently. Shelby, who believed in making her own way in the world, who thought it reprehensible to rely on connections and advantages of birth to get anything. Shelby, who never admitted her father was a state senator unless she was asked point-blank.

Shelby had pulled strings for him. Damn, she must be serious about this love stuff.

"We…we can't exactly just let him go," the gray-haired woman said, uncharacteristically flustered now. "He…he assaulted—"

"I know what he did, and I know why he did it. Are you people blind and deaf, too? And to think, I actually appointed you. What do you mean, you can't let him go? Haven't you ever heard of a pardon?"

"You're pardoning him?" the prosecutor asked.

"Isn't that what I just said?"

"For which crimes?"

"All of 'em!" The governor held out his hand. His assistant handed him a thick folder, which the governor then handed to the prosecutor. Then he pulled out a chair, recently vacated by some lawyer, and sat down. "I'll just sit right here. I want the young man home with his family tonight, and I'm not leaving this chair until it's a done deal."

Finally, the shocked silence lifted, and everyone started talking at once. Aides and assistants were sent scurrying to produce whatever paperwork was deemed necessary. Reporters talked on cell phones. Photographers snapped pictures.

And Gavin just sat there, numb, afraid that if he moved, if he spoke, it would all go away and he would find himself waking up in his cell in Huntsville, the whole thing a dream.

A few minutes later, a guard unlocked Gavin's shackles and removed them. He was shown into someone's hastily vacated office, where he was handed a set of clean clothes and told—respectfully, he thought—that he should change into them. When he emerged, Houseman was there to greet him with a big smile and the assurance that he was a free man.

"This is all highly irregular, mind you," Houseman said as he hustled Gavin down a back hallway. "I'm not even sure it's legal. But no one's going to argue with the governor of the State of Texas. I've got a car waiting in the garage. They've sealed it off from the press."

Gavin didn't argue. He wanted to get as far away from that court building as he could—before someone changed their mind.

A silver Lexus idled near the door from which they emerged into the garage. Houseman trotted up to it, opened the back door for Gavin, then jumped into the passenger seat. Gavin dived into the back seat and slammed the door, and the car screeched off.

It took him a few seconds to realize he wasn't alone in the back seat. Shelby was there, wearing a tremulous smile.

He'd wanted to talk to her so badly, but now he hardly knew what to say. *Thanks* just didn't seem to cover it.

"You're the governor's goddaughter?" he finally asked.

She nodded.

"He must be a very good friend to do what he did for you."

"No, Gavin, he's just a fair-minded man. Yeah, I pulled some strings to get your case in front of him. But once he reviewed the facts, he was incensed. He felt everyone was grandstanding for the sake of publicity. The District Attorney is up for reelection, and he wants to be seen as tough on crime. I knew Governor Wilson was considering some type of intervention. But even the governor can't go against what the parole board recommends."

"How did he do what he did, then?" Gavin asked.

"He did a little grandstanding of his own," Houseman interjected with a laugh. "I'm not even sure he's allowed to pardon you for crimes you haven't been convicted of. But my guess is all charges will be quietly dropped. No one seemed inclined to object to your immediate release, not with the cameras rolling and the media playing the local-hero angle for all it's worth."

Gavin reached over and took Shelby's hand. "You really went out on a limb for me. I can't believe you admitted before God and everybody that we're…um… involved."

"Oddly enough, that's the only lie I told. We aren't involved—at least, not anymore. Not according to you, anyway." She drew her hand away from his hold and laid it in her lap.

Gavin shot a nervous glance toward the front seat, where Houseman and the driver listened with acute interest they didn't even bother to hide. "Could we talk about this later?"

"No," she said, thrusting her chin out belligerently. "I want to talk about it right now. Do you want me or not?"

"You know I want you—more than anything. But I also want you to be happy."

"You think that loving you doesn't make me happy? Gavin, it's the only thing that's kept me going these last few weeks. After all the death I've seen, the downright evil—knowing there are good people in the world, and that one of those people cared enough about me to risk his life and his freedom—that's what kept me from packing up my things, grabbing Jake and running away. You make me happy, Gavin, and even if you had to spend the rest of your life in prison, I could not stop loving you."

Gavin was speechless. How could she speak of such personal things with absolutely no apology, no embarrassment?

"So now you're a free man with a bright future ahead of you and no restrictions on where or how you live. You could even become a cop again. You have no excuses anymore. If you turn me away now, it has to be because you don't love me. So what's it gonna be?"

Gavin couldn't begin to articulate the million things he wanted to say to Shelby, so he didn't even try. He hauled her into his arms and kissed her the way she was meant to be kissed, smearing her lipstick, mussing her hair, disheveling her clothes. And for the first time, he felt no guilt, no shame, not even a fleeting sense that he was doing wrong by her, dishonoring her in some way. He felt only a strong sense of rightness—and a surge of desire for her that nearly made him pass out.

When he paused to catch his breath, she smiled. "Good answer."

* * * * *

Look for the next book by Kara Lennox,
THE FORGOTTEN COWBOY,
on sale in January 2005,
only from Harlequin American Romance.

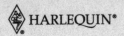

HARLEQUIN®

INTRIGUE®

presents brand-new installments of

HEROES, INC.

from *USA TODAY* bestselling author
Susan Kearney

HIJACKED HONEYMOON
(HI #808, November 2004)

PROTECTOR S.O.S.
(HI #814, December 2004)

Available at your favorite retail outlet.

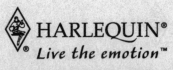

HARLEQUIN®
Live the emotion™

www.eHarlequin.com

HIHI2

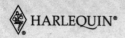
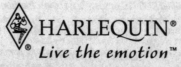

If you enjoyed what you just read,
then we've got an offer you can't resist!

Take 2 bestselling love stories FREE!

Plus get a FREE surprise gift!

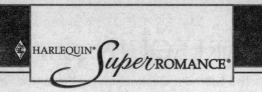

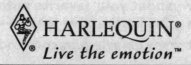

HARLEQUIN®
INTRIGUE®

Someone had infiltrated the insular realm of the Colby Agency....

INTERNAL AFFAIRS

The line between attraction and protection has vanished in these two brand-new investigations.

Look for these back-to-back books by

DEBRA WEBB

October 2004
SITUATION: OUT OF CONTROL

November 2004
PRIORITY: FULL EXPOSURE

Available at your favorite retail outlet.

HARLEQUIN®
Live the emotion™

www.eHarlequin.com

like a phantom in the night
comes an exciting promotion from

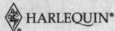
HARLEQUIN®

INTRIGUE

GOTHIC ROMANCE

Look for a provocative
gothic-themed thriller each month
by your favorite Intrigue authors!
Once you surrender to the classic
blend of chilling suspense and
electrifying romance in these
gripping page-turners, there will
be no turning back.…

Available wherever Harlequin books are sold.

HARLEQUIN®
Live the emotion™

www.eHarlequin.com

HIE3